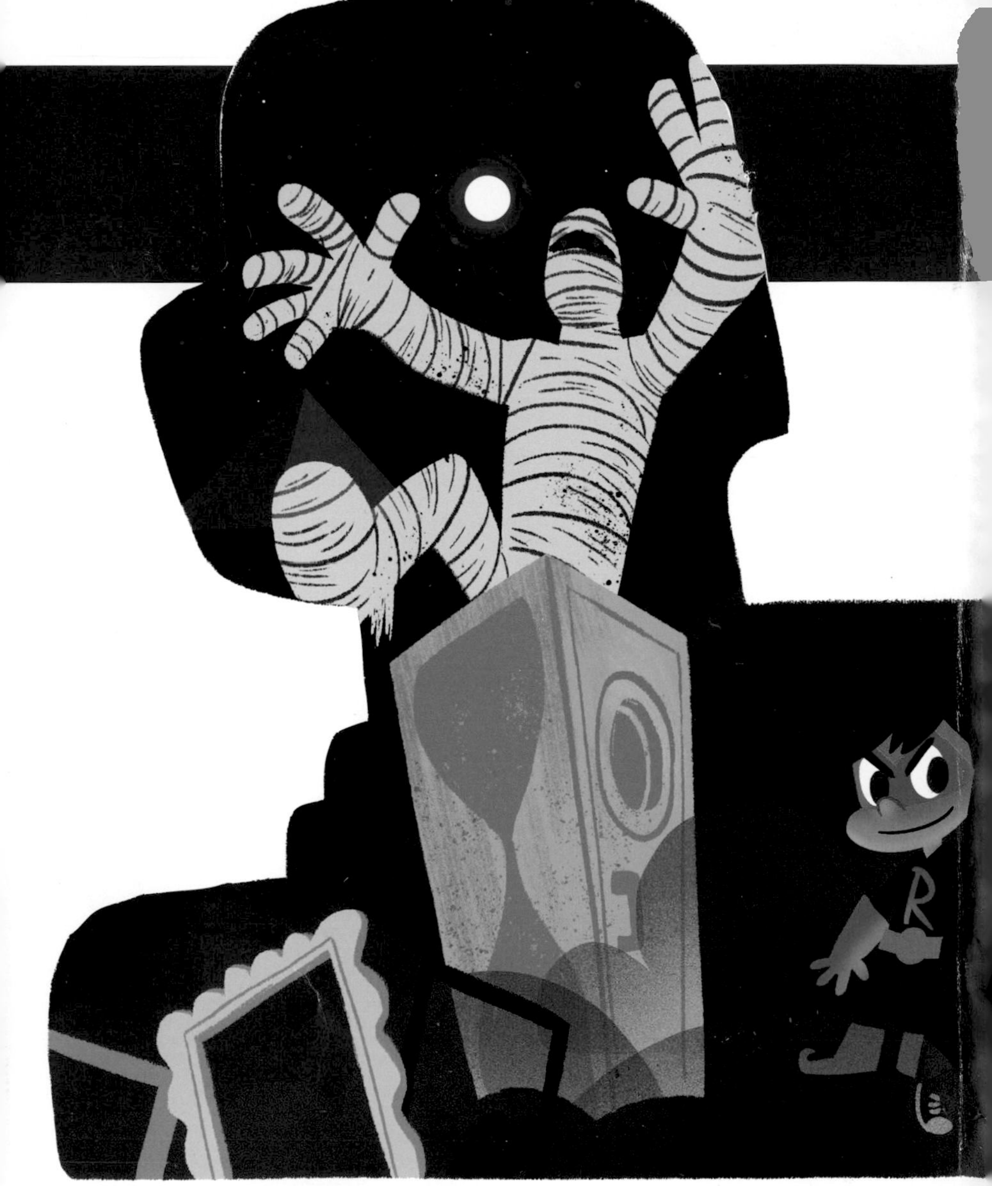
R

COOL SCHOOL

DREW PENDOUS

#2

Travels to Ancient Egypt

adapted by
David Lewman
based on the screenplay
by **Rachel O. Crouse**

illustrated by
Robert Dress
art direction by
Dan Markowitz

based on the series
COOL SCHOOL
and characters created by
Rob Kurtz

STERLING CHILDREN'S BOOKS
New York

STERLING CHILDREN'S BOOKS
New York

An Imprint of Sterling Publishing Co., Inc.
1166 Avenue of the Americas
New York, NY 10036

ISBN 978-1-4549-3109-6

Distributed in Canada by Sterling Publishing Co., Inc.
c/o Canadian Manda Group, 664 Annette Street
Toronto, Ontario M6S 2C8, Canada
Distributed in the United Kingdom by GMC Distribution Services
Castle Place, 166 High Street, Lewes, East Sussex BN7 1XU, England
Distributed in Australia by NewSouth Books
University of New South Wales, Sydney, NSW 2052, Australia

For information about custom editions, special sales, and premium and corporate purchases, please contact Sterling Special Sales at 800-805-5489 or specialsales@sterlingpublishing.com.

Manufactured in China

Lot #:
2 4 6 8 10 9 7 5 3 1
01/19

sterlingpublishing.com

CONTENTS

CHAPTER ONE

YES, it's time for another ***amazing*** ***adventure*** starring everyone's favorite superhero . . .

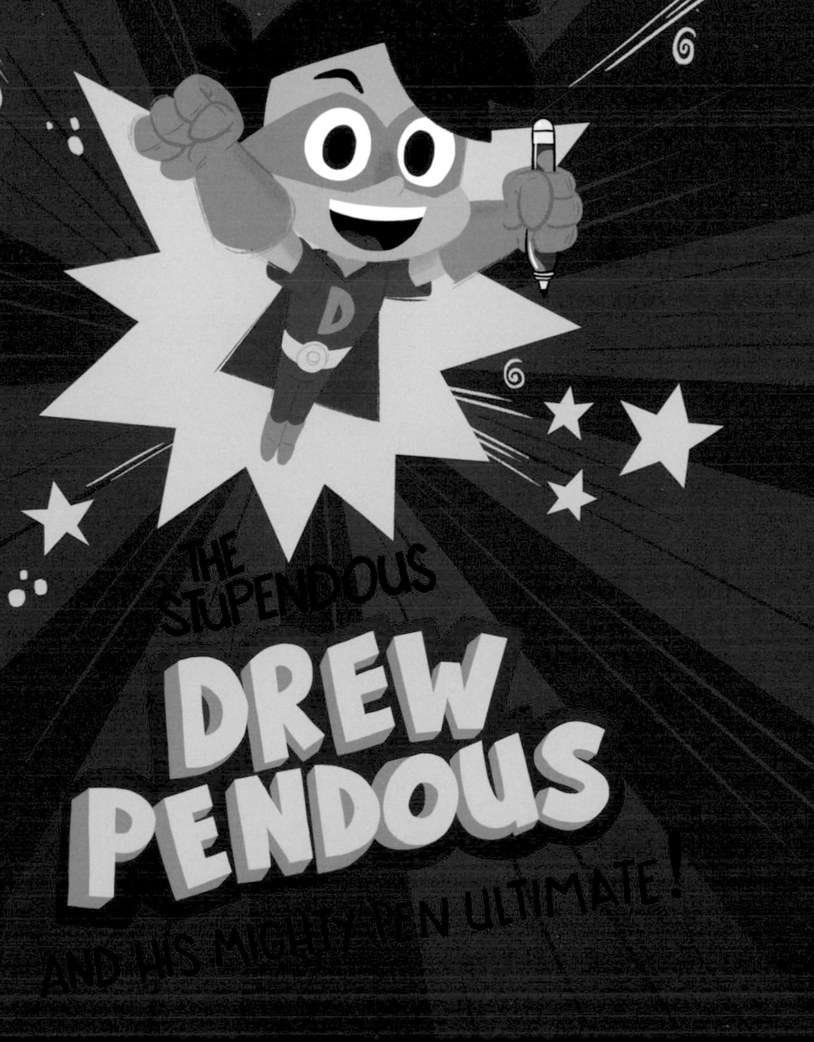
THE STUPENDOUS
DREW PENDOUS
AND HIS MIGHTY PEN ULTIMATE!

It was the start of another cool day at Cool School! But Ms. Booksy had an announcement: "Today, we will not have class here at Cool School."

"Awwww!" everybody groaned.

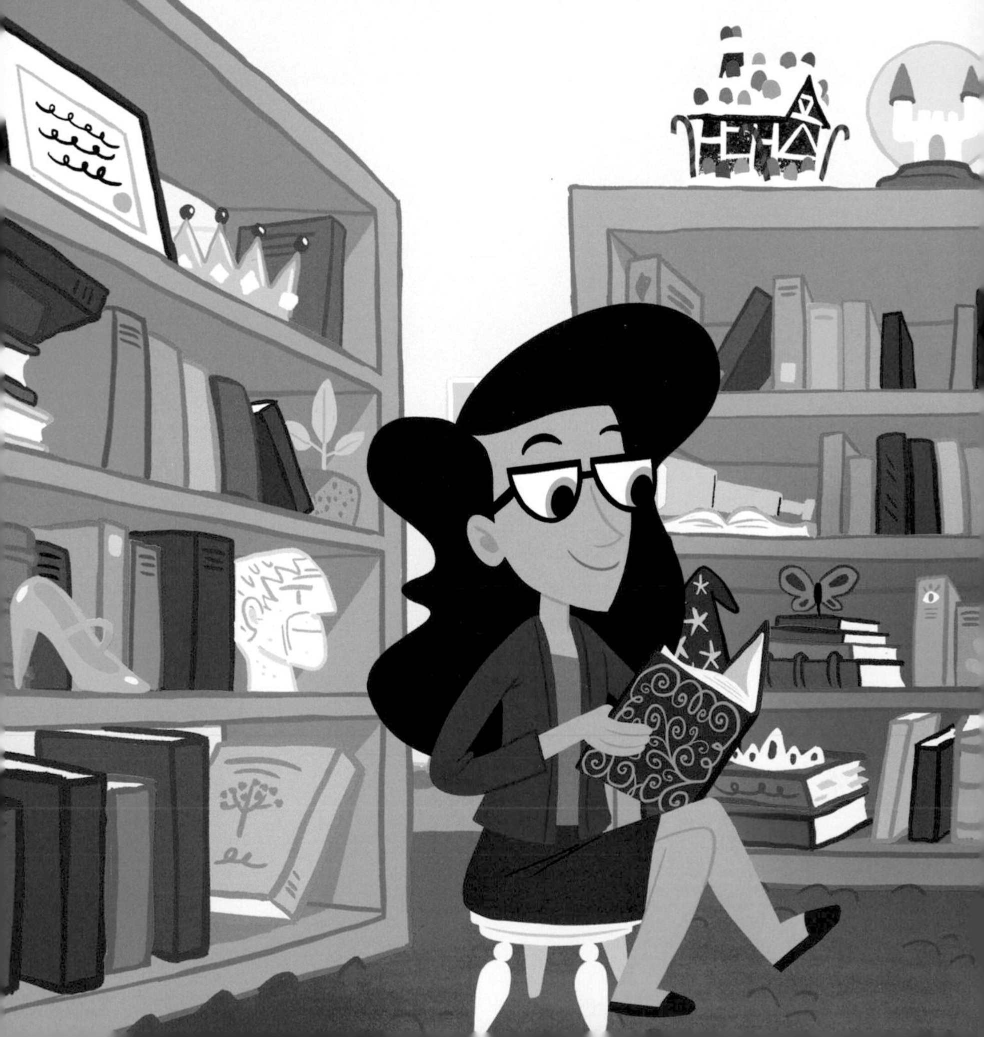

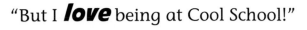
"But I **love** being at Cool School!"
Drew said. He raised his hand.

"Yes, Drew?" Ms. Booksy said.

"Ms. Booksy, why aren't we having class
here today?" Drew asked.

"Because today we are going on a **_field trip_** to the museum!" Ms. Booksy explained.

"YAY!" all the students cheered.

They **_LOVED_** field trips to the museum. It had all kinds of cool things— **_paintings_**

and **rocks** and **costumes** and **statues**

and **dinosaur skeletons** and lots of **other cool stuff!**

So they all climbed onto yellow Cool School buses and rode to the museum. They got there just as the museum was opening up for the day.

Let's see. . . . Who went on the field trip to the museum that day?

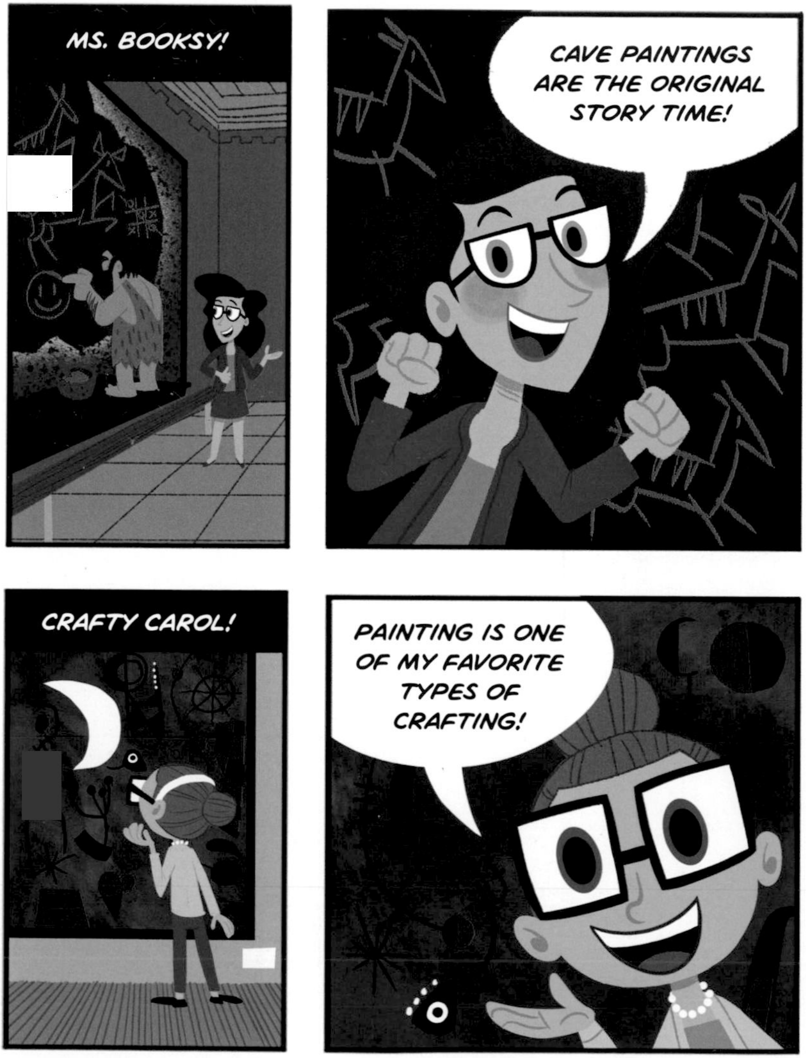
MS. BOOKSY!
CAVE PAINTINGS ARE THE ORIGINAL STORY TIME!
CRAFTY CAROL!
PAINTING IS ONE OF MY FAVORITE TYPES OF CRAFTING!

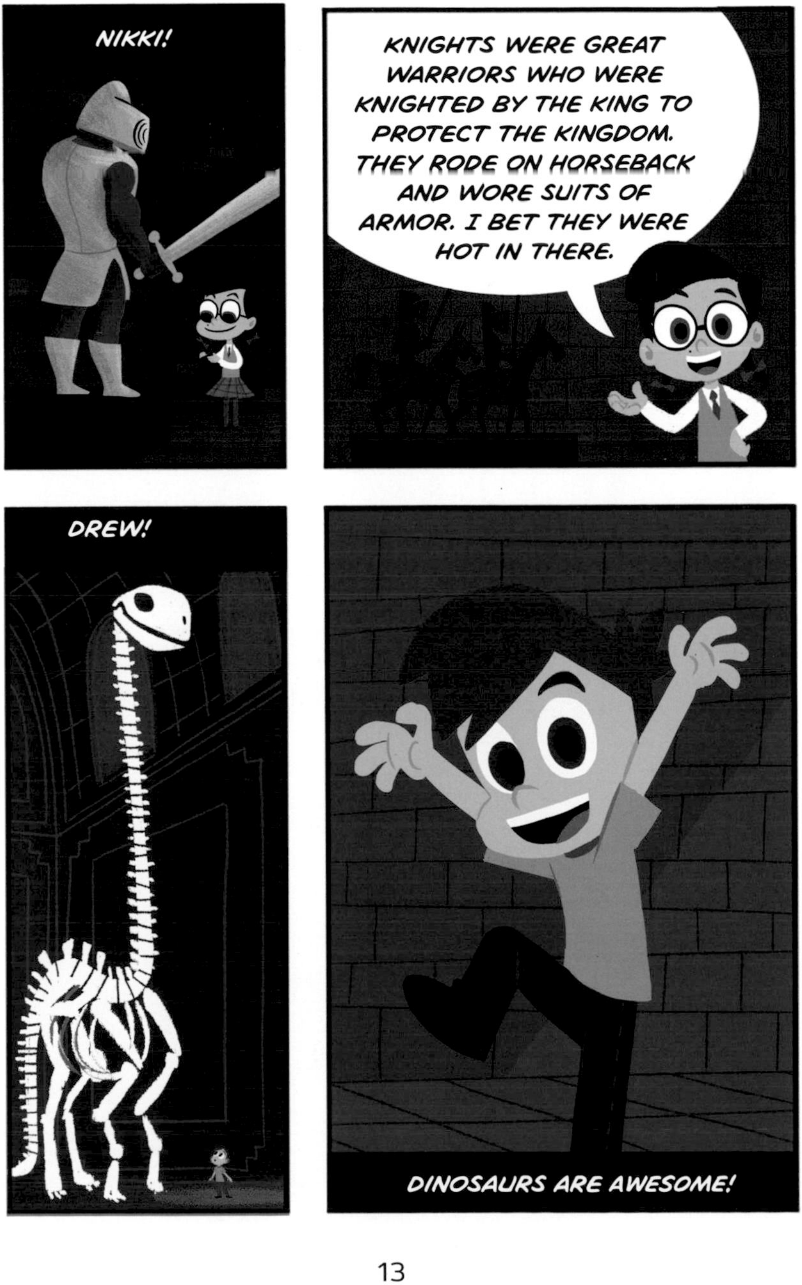
NIKKI!
KNIGHTS WERE GREAT WARRIORS WHO WERE KNIGHTED BY THE KING TO PROTECT THE KINGDOM. THEY RODE ON HORSEBACK AND WORE SUITS OF ARMOR. I BET THEY WERE HOT IN THERE.
DREW!
DINOSAURS ARE AWESOME!

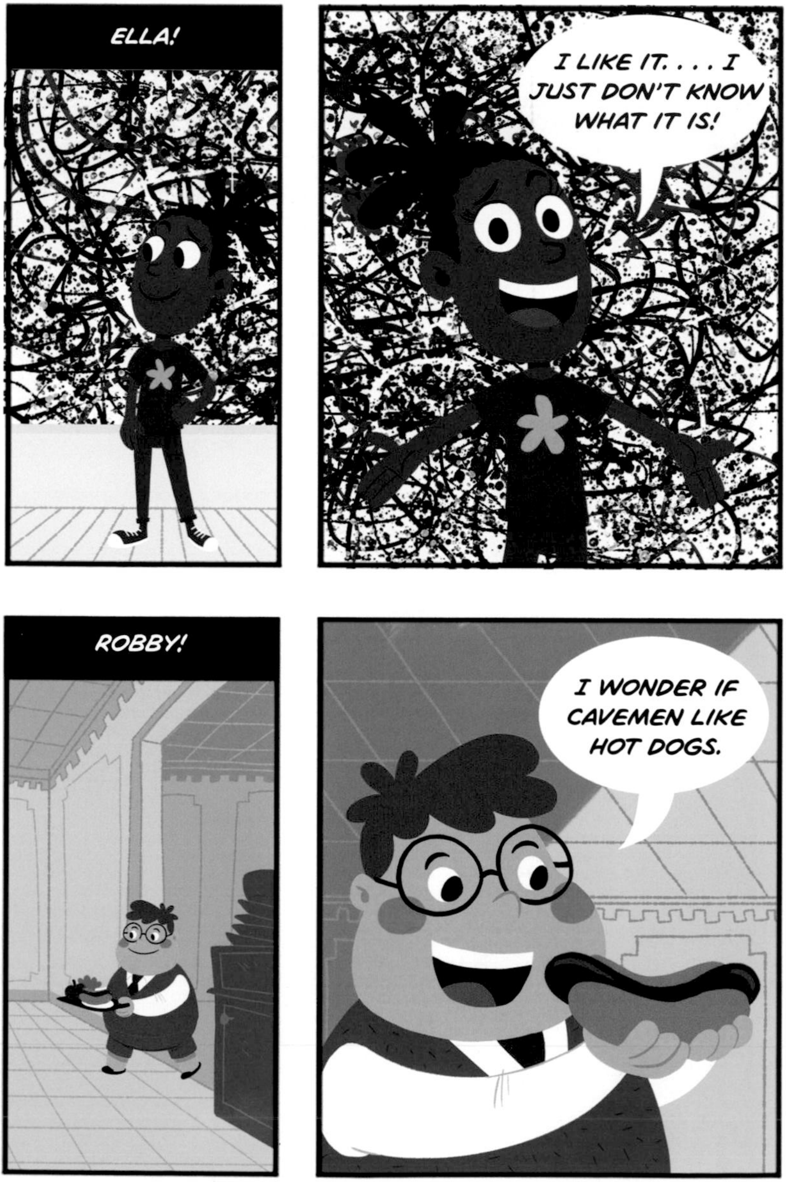
ELLA!
I LIKE IT. . . . I JUST DON'T KNOW WHAT IT IS!
ROBBY!
I WONDER IF CAVEMEN LIKE HOT DOGS.

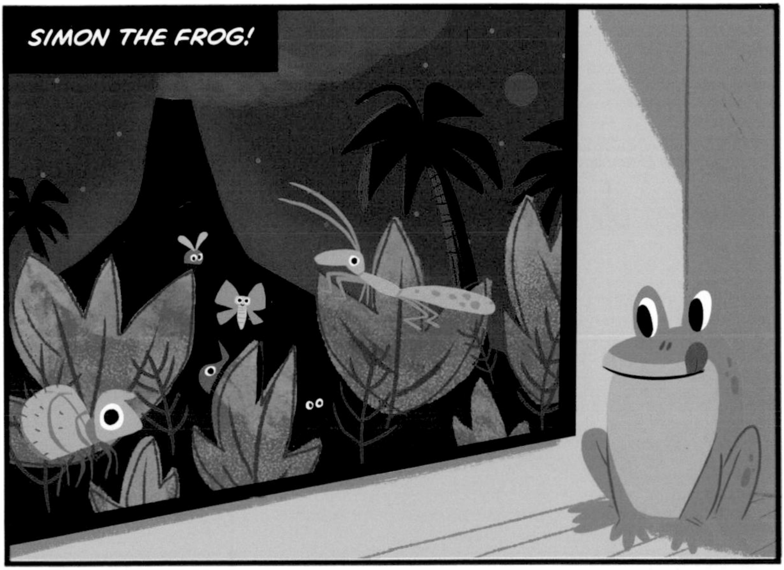
SIMON THE FROG!

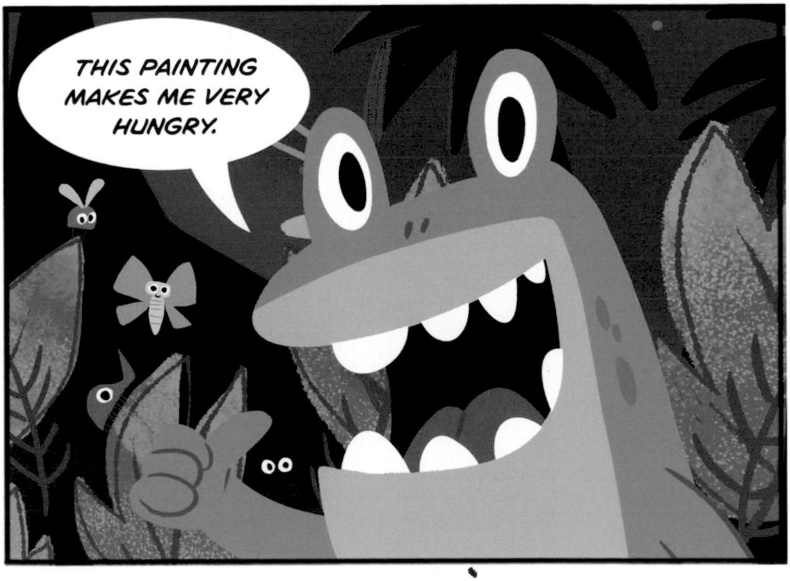
THIS PAINTING MAKES ME VERY HUNGRY.

Drew was having a great time! He and Robby went into the museum's Hall of Ancient Egypt. "Hey, Robby," Drew said. "What's a ***mummy's*** favorite type of music?"

"I don't know," Robby said, thinking. "What is it?"

"Rap music!" Drew said, laughing. "Get it? *Rap?*"

"Ha!" Robby said. "Good one, Drew."

Then they heard a ***creepy*** voice moan,

"DREWWWWW WHO'S YOUR MUMMY?"

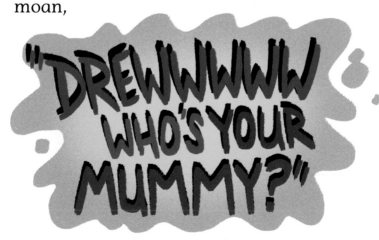

They turned and saw a mummy staggering toward them, wrapped all in bandages!

"AAAAHHH!"

Robby screamed. "The mummy! It's ***alive!"***

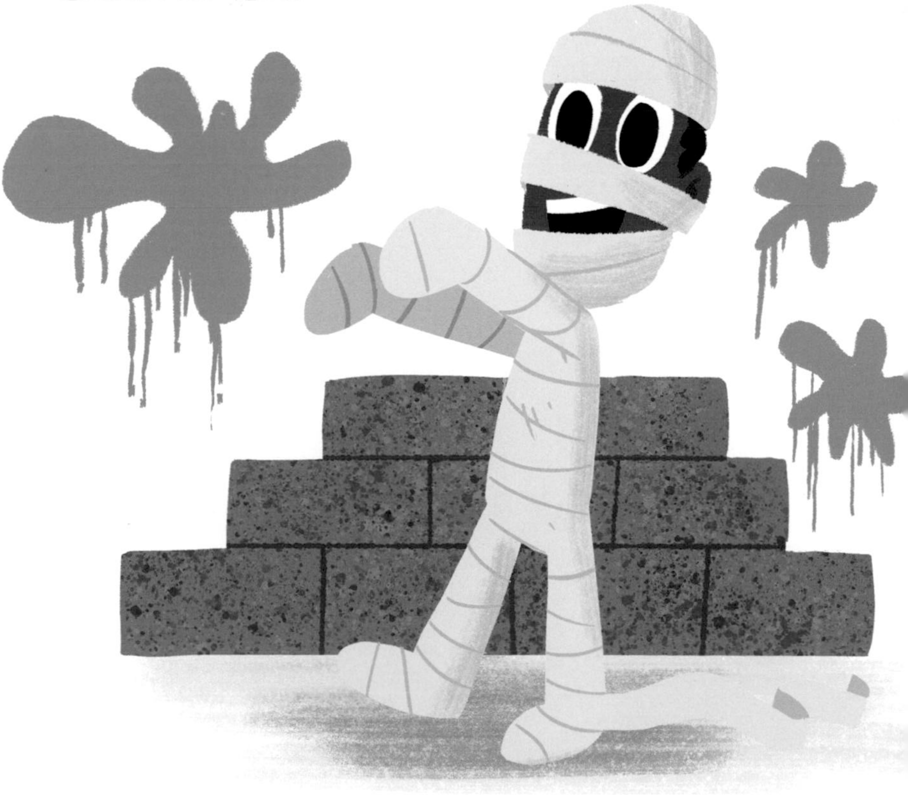

CHAPTER TWO

DREW GIGGLED. That confused Robby. Why was Drew giggling? Shouldn't he be screaming?

RIP! The mummy ***tore off all its bandages***. They floated down to the ground, and Robby noticed that they weren't bandages at all—they were ***toilet paper***! What kind of mummy is wrapped in toilet paper?

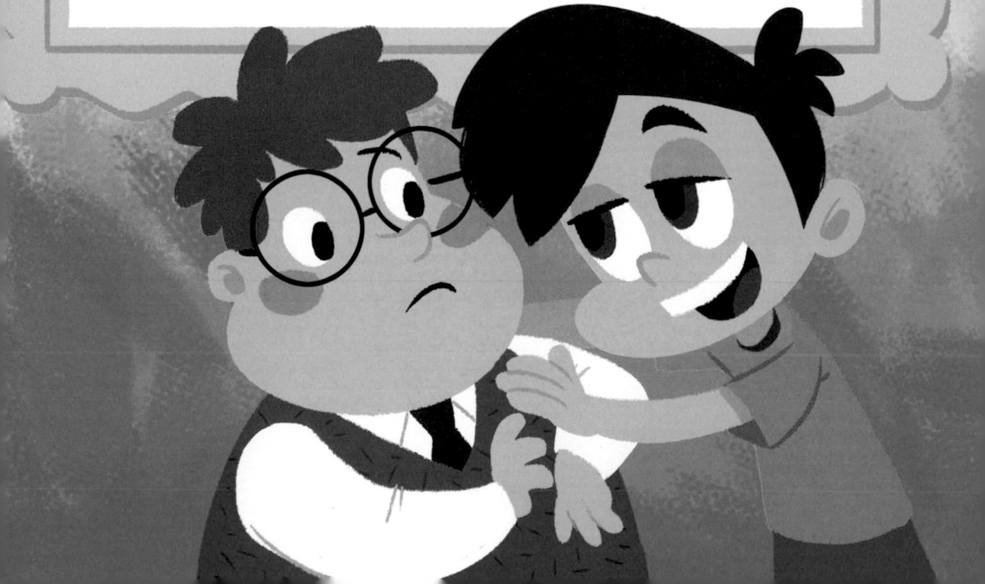

A fake one. It wasn't really a mummy at all! It was . . .

. . . Ella!

"Ha ha ha!" she laughed. "You should have seen your face!" She imitated Robby's scream.

"AAAH! IT'S ALIVE!" Ella laughed again. "You wouldn't survive a day in real Egypt!"

"He-he," Drew giggled. "I knew it was you, Ella! I recognized your **purple shoes!"**

"Not funny, Ella!" Robby said. "You know, you're not supposed to ***mess with mummies!*** They'll come back to haunt you!" He looked down at Ella's purple shoes. "Some even steal your ***favorite sneakers!"***

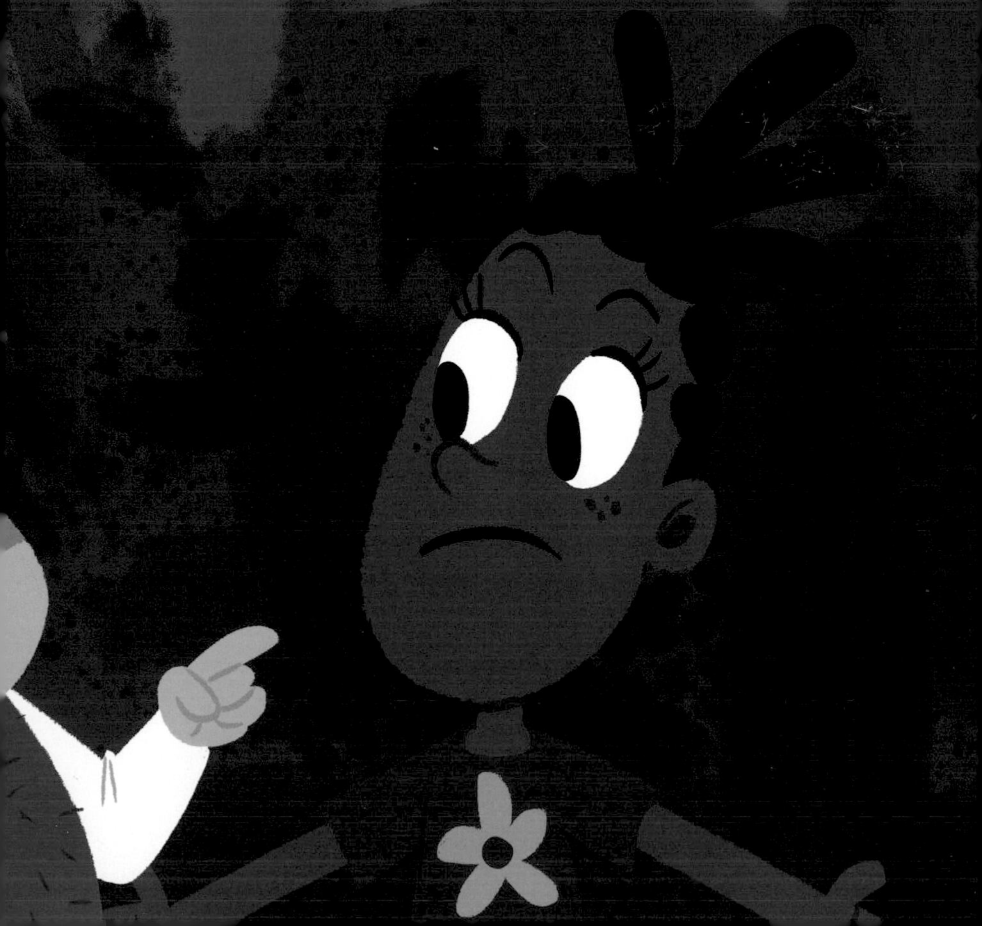

"I'll **share** my sneakers with a **mummy** any day!" Ella said bravely. **"They don't scare me!"**

Nikki called to them from a big room with glass walls. **"Hey, guys, look!"**

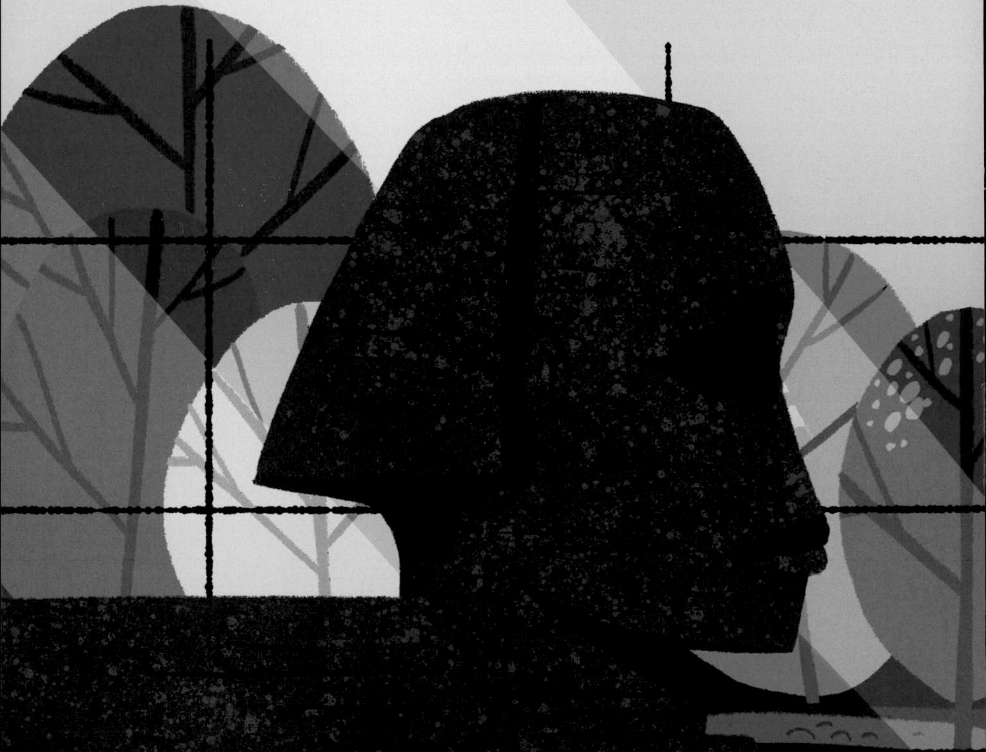

Drew, Ella, and Robby hurried over to see what Nikki wanted to show them. The room had a ***big statue*** in it ***carved out of stone.*** It looked like a lion with a human head.

"It's a replica of the famous ***Egyptian Great Sphinx of Giza!"*** Nikki said. "And what I read is true—the ***nose*** is ***missing."***

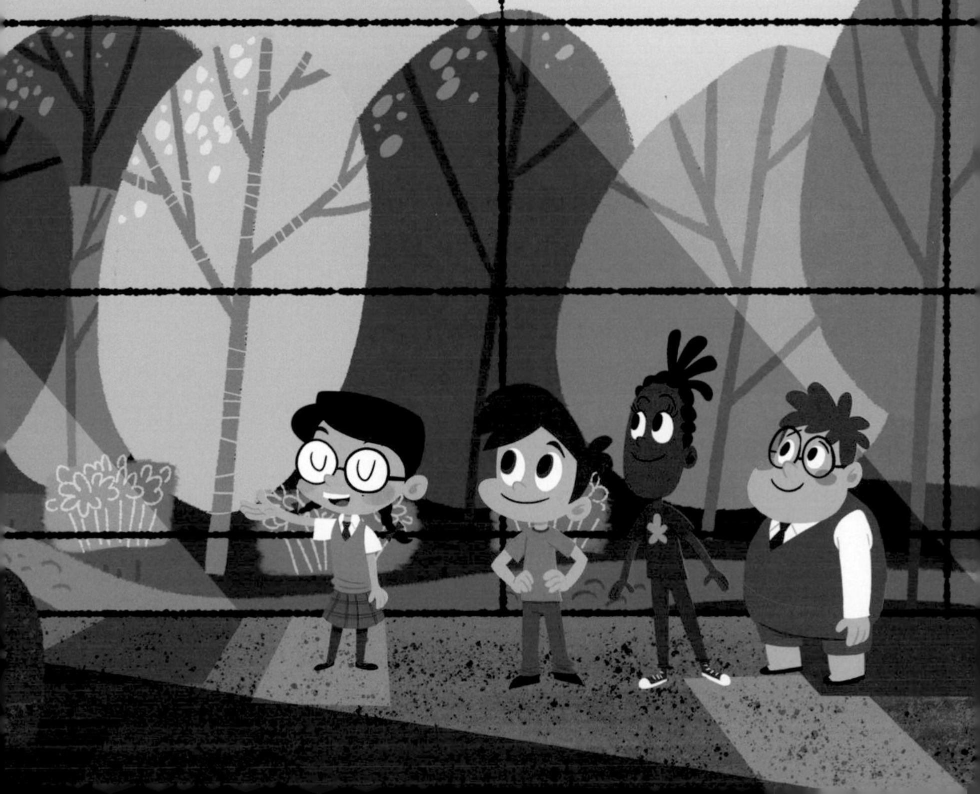

Drew looked up at the Sphinx's face. Sure enough, **the nose was broken off**.

"Legend has it that the Sphinx's **missing nose is still hidden** somewhere in Egypt," Nikki continued. "And whoever **finds** the nose will be **granted any wish** they want!"

A **wish** sounded pretty great to Drew.

"No way!" he said. "Like **a trip** to the Bahamas? Or **world peace?** Or a new **video game?"**

"Yep," Nikki said, nodding. **"Anything you like!** That's the rumor, anyway."

Crafty Carol peeked back through the doorway to the next gallery. "All right, kids! **Come on!** Time for the ***next exhibit!***"

Nikki, Robby, and Ella headed out of the Egyptian exhibit. But ***Drew hung back,*** thinking. . . .

CHAPTER THREE

HM, DREW thought. *The legend of the missing nose does sound cool. I've always wanted to go to Egypt. Maybe if I just . . .*

He took out his trusty Pen Ultimate and drew a *D* on his chest. That turned him into . . . ***SUPER DREW!*** Everyone's favorite superhero!

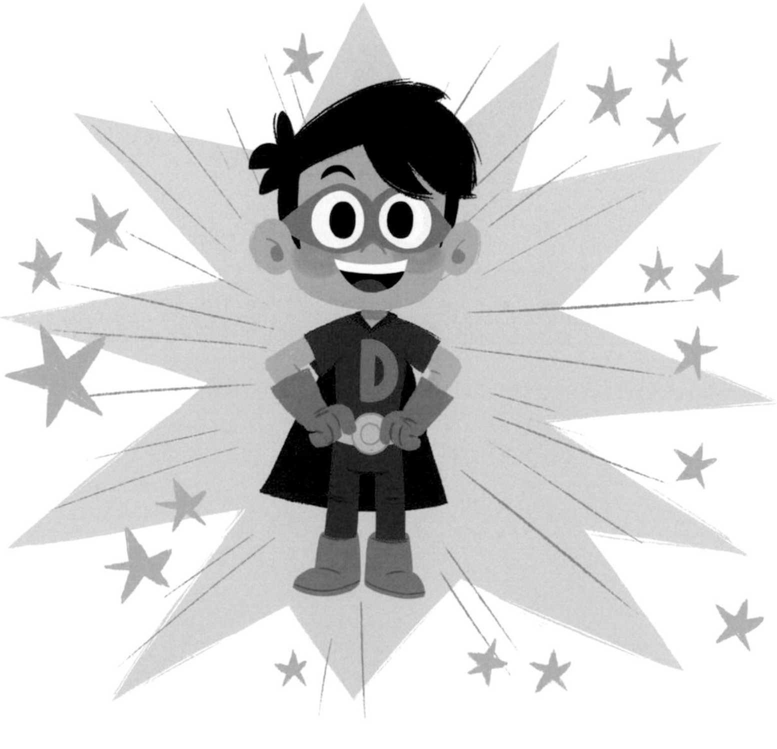
D

Still using his **Pen Ultimate,** Drew quickly sketched the awesomest *time machine* ever. It had tons of mysterious dials and buttons and a door so you could go inside to ***travel through time***.

Drew dashed inside his time machine, ready to go back to ***ancient Egypt***. But before he could leave, Ella came looking for him. ***"Drew!"*** she called. "We're all waiting for you!"

She noticed the time machine with its **big hourglass** drawn on the side. "Hey!" she said. **"What's going on here?"**

Drew popped back out of his time machine. "Oh, uh, **I was just, uh, hanging out.** In this um . . . time machine."

Ella looked amazed. **"Whoa!** You're going back in time to ancient Egypt to **track down the missing nose**

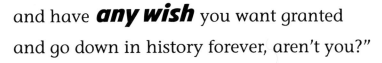

and have ***any wish*** you want granted and go down in history forever, aren't you?"

Ella was very good at guessing what people had planned.

"Uh, ***maybe . . . kinda . . . okay, yes,"*** Drew said.

"Well, not without me, you're not!" Ella announced.

So Drew and Ella got in the time machine together.

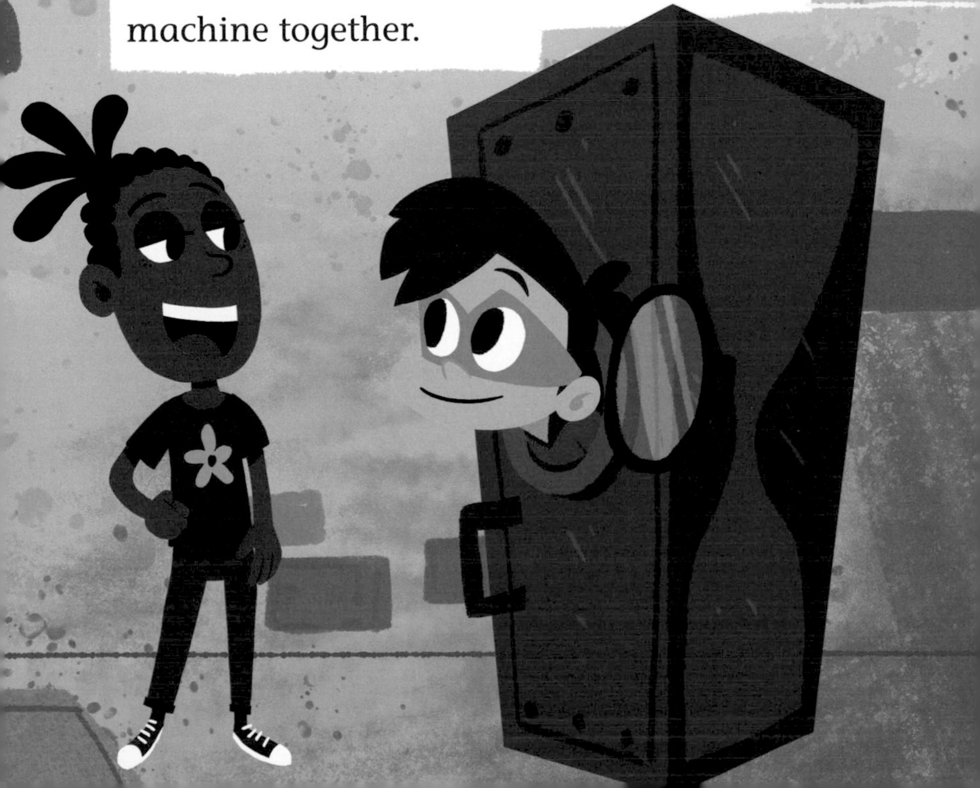

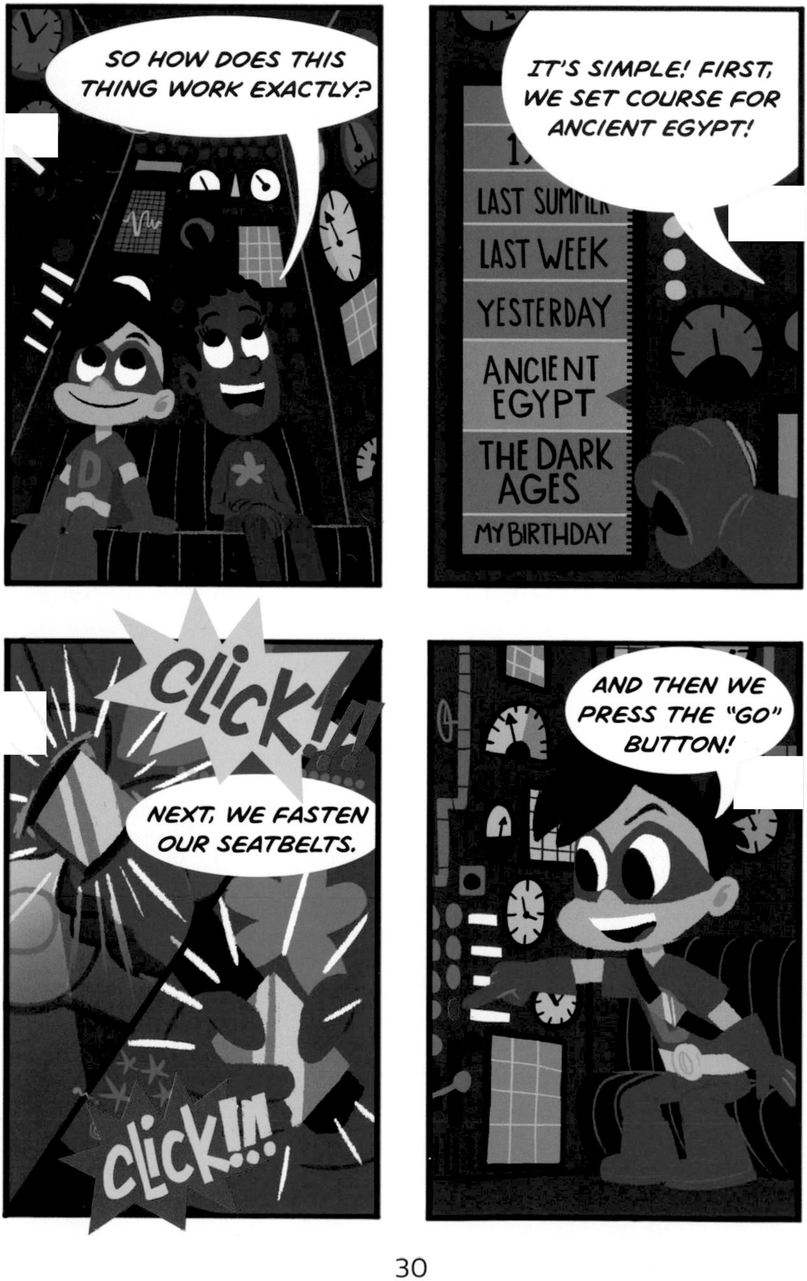
SO HOW DOES THIS THING WORK EXACTLY?
IT'S SIMPLE! FIRST, WE SET COURSE FOR ANCIENT EGYPT!
LAST WEEK
YESTERDAY
ANCIENT EGYPT
THE DARK AGES
MY BIRTHDAY
CLICK!!!
NEXT, WE FASTEN OUR SEATBELTS.
CLICK!!!
AND THEN WE PRESS THE "GO" BUTTON!

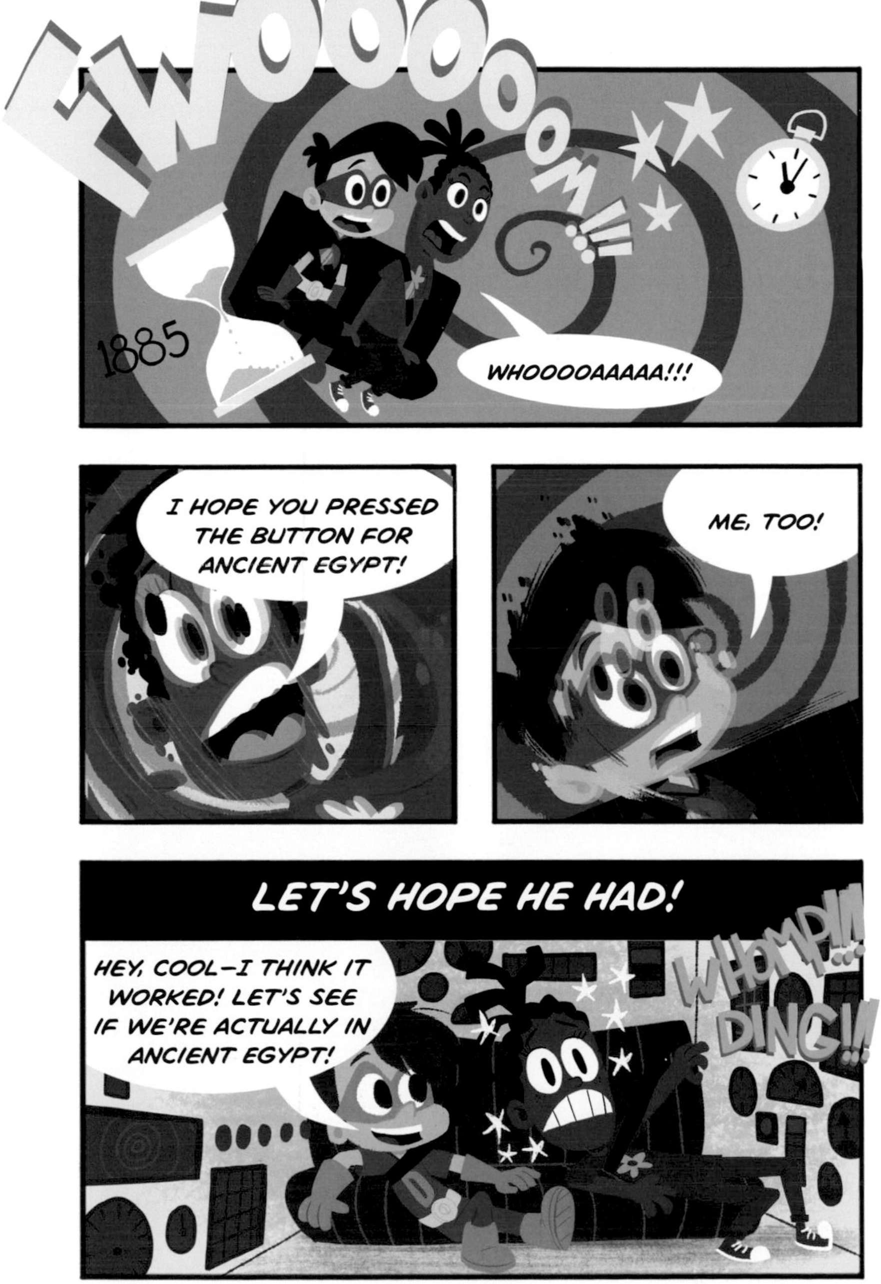
FWOOOOOM!!!
1885
WHOOOOAAAAA!!!
I HOPE YOU PRESSED THE BUTTON FOR ANCIENT EGYPT!
ME, TOO!
LET'S HOPE HE HAD!
HEY, COOL—I THINK IT WORKED! LET'S SEE IF WE'RE ACTUALLY IN ANCIENT EGYPT!
WHOMP!!!
DING!!!

CHAPTER FOUR

DREW PUSHED the time machine's door open. He and Ella saw ***palms trees*** and lots of ***sand . . .*** and the ***Great Sphinx!*** It was still being built! ***They were in ancient Egypt!***

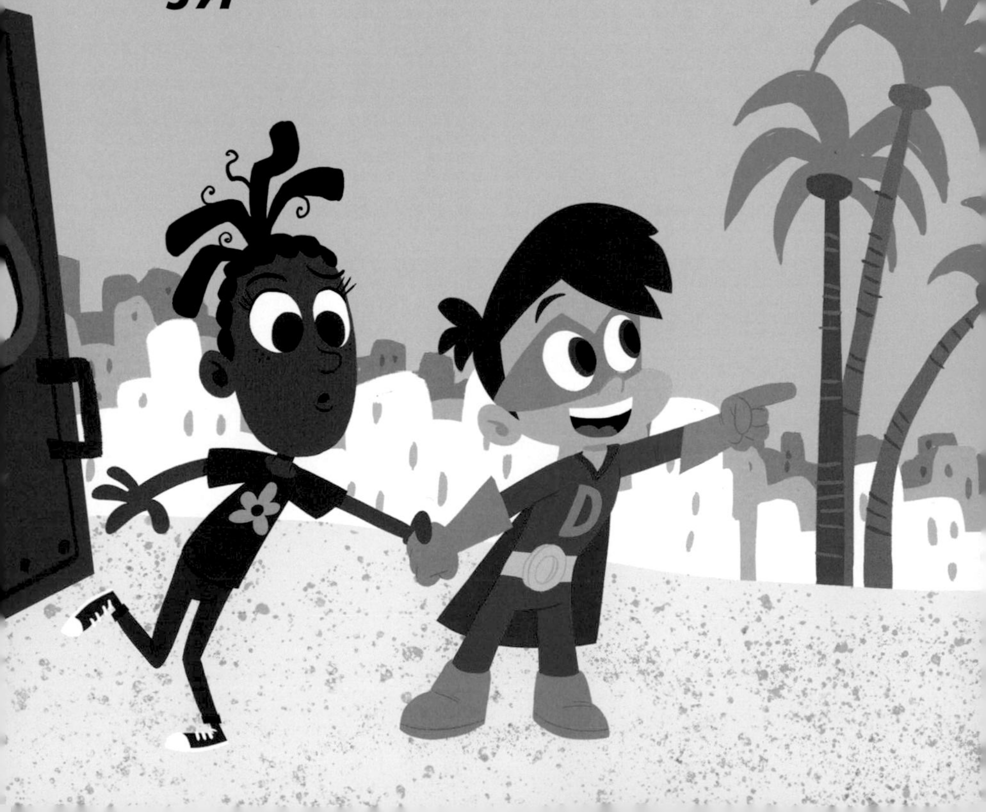

"Your *time machine worked!*"
Ella said.

"*Of course it worked!*" Drew
said. "*Come on!* Let's check out ancient
Egypt!"

They hurried out of the time machine
and ran through the sand toward the
Sphinx. "*Hey, look!*" Drew said,
pointing. "*It's still got its nose!*
Hmm, that was easy. I guess *we
found it.*"

"Wow," Ella said. "The Sphinx looks great! I wish everyone could see how much better it looks with its nose!"

They saw **two young Egyptians,** a boy and a girl.

"Hello!" Drew said.

"Hi!" Ella said, waving. **"Can you tell us anything about the Sphinx?"**

"Oh, yes!" the boy said, excited. "We are happy to tell you anything you'd like to know!"

"Okay," Drew said, thinking. "Like, um, **what is it?"**

"The Sphinx is **a monument to the pharaoh,"** the girl explained.

"What's a **pharaoh?"** Ella asked.

"The pharaoh is our leader," the boy said. "The Sphinx has the **body** of a **lion** and the **head** of the **pharaoh.**"

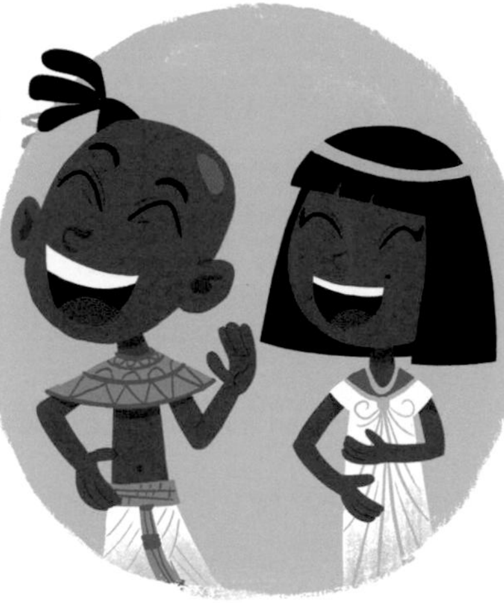

Ella looked doubtful. "I'm sure your leader is really smart," she said, "but I doubt his head is ***that*** big!"

The boy and the girl laughed.

"What's ***all that wood*** around the Sphinx?" Drew asked. "Is it some kind of fence to keep people out?"

"No," the girl said, shaking her head. "It's called ***scaffolding***. The workers who are building the Sphinx out of limestone use the scaffolding ***to climb up*** onto the top of the monument."

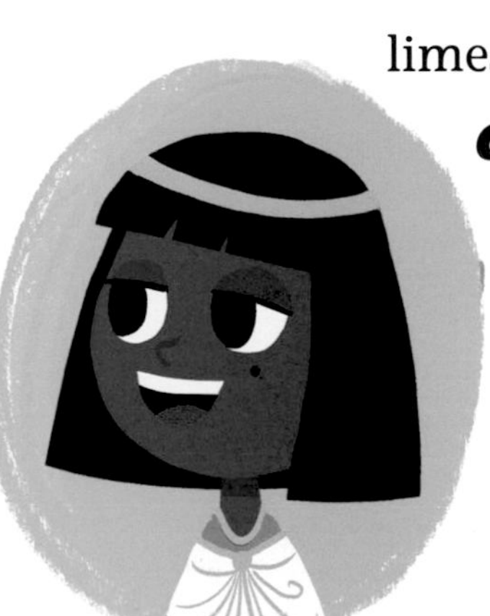

"Kind of ***like a ladder?"*** Ella said. "Or ***stairs?"***

"Exactly!" the girl said.

Drew noticed something. **"Hey, look! Up there!"** he said, pointing to the top of the Sphinx's head.

"What is it?" Ella asked.

"It looks like **a person wearing a cape,"** Drew said.

The Egyptian boy shaded his eyes,

peering at the shadowy figure on top of the Sphinx. "That's odd," he said. "All the workers are on break right now. No one is working."

"That doesn't look like one of the workers," the girl said.

Drew looked determined. ***"Uh-oh,*** we'd better check this out! And I know just what to do!" He whipped out his ***Pen Ultimate*** and started to draw. When he was finished, Ella looked surprised.

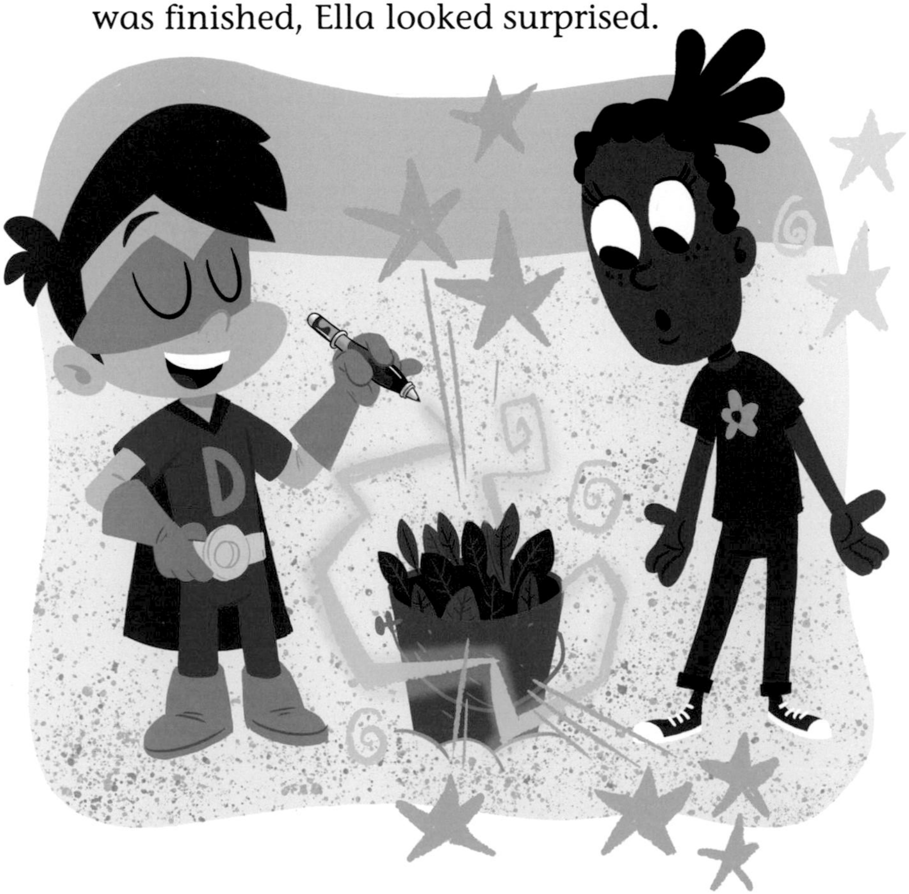

"You drew a bucket full of dried leaves?" she asked, confused.

"Exactly!" Drew said. **_"Camels love dry leaves!"_**

He was right. In no time at all, a camel had hurried across the sand to the bucket full of leaves, stuck its head in, and started eating. **_MUNCH! CRUNCH!_**

While the camel was happily munching, Drew and Ella climbed up onto its back. They sat down, holding onto the camel's two humps.

"Uh, you don't fly, do you?" Drew asked the camel.

"Of course not!" Ella said. "**Camels can't fly!** They don't have wings!"

"Good point," Drew said. Using his **Pen Ultimate,** he **drew wings** on the camel. "There!" he said. "Come on, camel! **Fly us up to the top of the Sphinx!"**

The camel took its head out of the bucket, ***flapped its new wings,*** and took off flying!

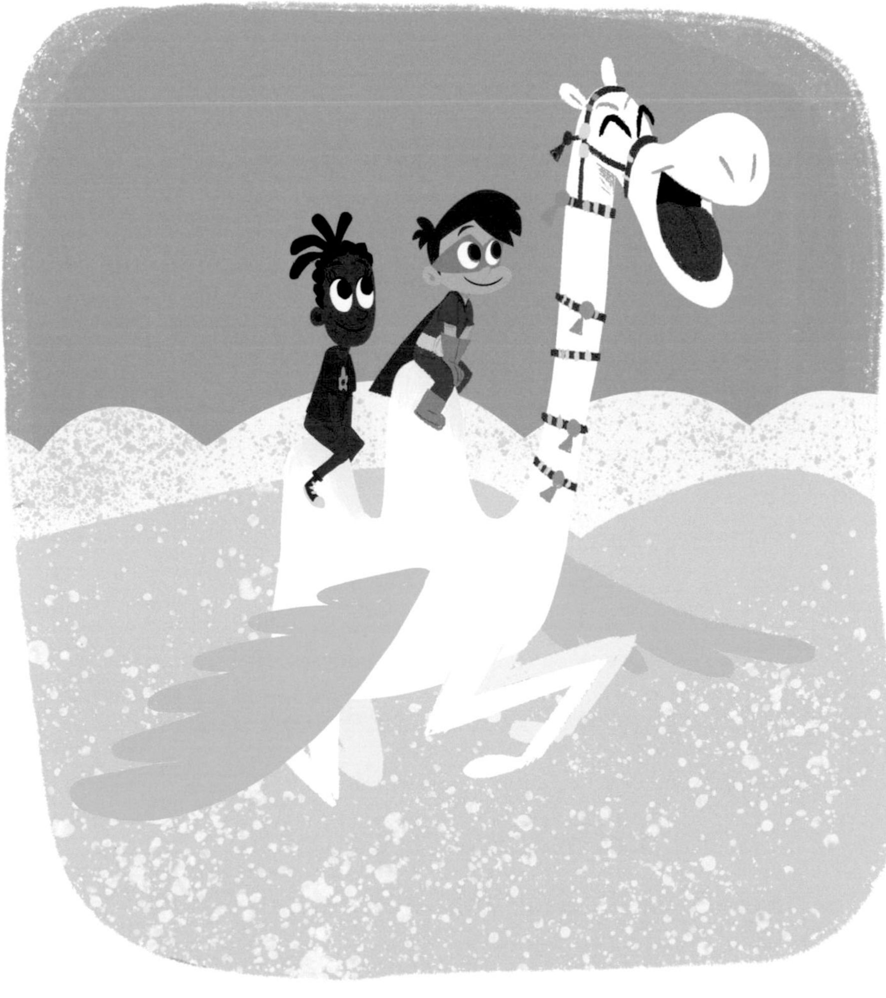

CHAPTER FIVE

THE FLYING CAMEL took Drew and Ella right up to the top of the Sphinx. Along the way, they passed by the nose.

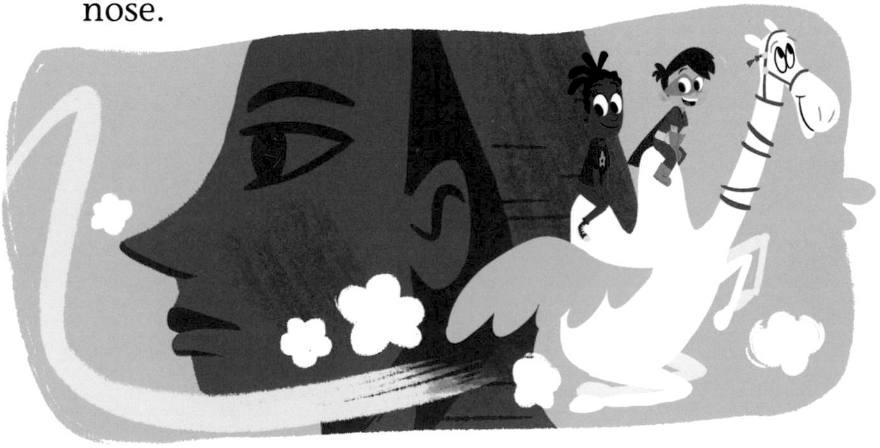

"Yep," Drew said, "the nose is definitely there. I wonder why it was missing in the museum?"

When they reached the top of the Sphinx's head, they saw none other than

RAY BLANK!!!

DREW'S EVIL TWIN!

"Ray Blank?!" Drew said. "I should've known he was behind the mystery of the missing nose!"

"But the nose **ISN'T** missing!" Ella said. "We just flew right by it!"

"I know," Drew said. "Time travel is kind of confusing."

The camel landed on the Sphinx's head, and Drew and Ella jumped down from the camel's back. "All right, Ray," Drew said. **"Hold it right there!"**

But Ray **DIDN'T** hold it right there!
Laughing his raspy, evil laugh, he flew off
the top of the Sphinx and down to its nose.
He hovered in the air right in front of the
nose. Then he took out . . .

. . . *his Magic Eraser!*

"What's that in his hand?" Ella asked.

"It's his Magic Eraser!" Drew answered. "Ray can use it to erase just about anything!"

Those words were barely out of Drew's mouth when Ray started to erase the nose off the Sphinx. ***"Ha ha ha!"*** he laughed as the nose disappeared.

"Stop right there, Evil Ray!"

Drew shouted. "You can't just erase noses off of sphinxes! That's super **NOT** cool!"

Ray flew up above the Sphinx's head and hovered over them. "How would **YOU** know what's cool, Doo Poopus?" he jeered. "With my **Magic Eraser,** I'm going to erase **ALL KINDS** of important things from history! This is just the beginning!"

"Wow," Ella said. "You really **ARE** evil!" Drew started slowly moving back toward the flying camel. ***"Wrong, Evil Ray!"***

he said. "This isn't the beginning! This is the **_END_** of you erasing important stuff! Like noses!"

"Oh, yeah?" Ray sneered. **_"Who's going to stop me?"_**

"WE ARE!" Drew said, jumping on the camel's back. "Come on, Ella!" He stretched out his hand to his friend. She took it, and Drew pulled her up onto the camel. The camel flapped its wings and they flew up into the air, straight toward Evil Ray.

"You'll never catch me!" Ray crowed as he took off flying. They chased him around the Sphinx three times until suddenly he flew straight down into a dark tunnel that led underground!

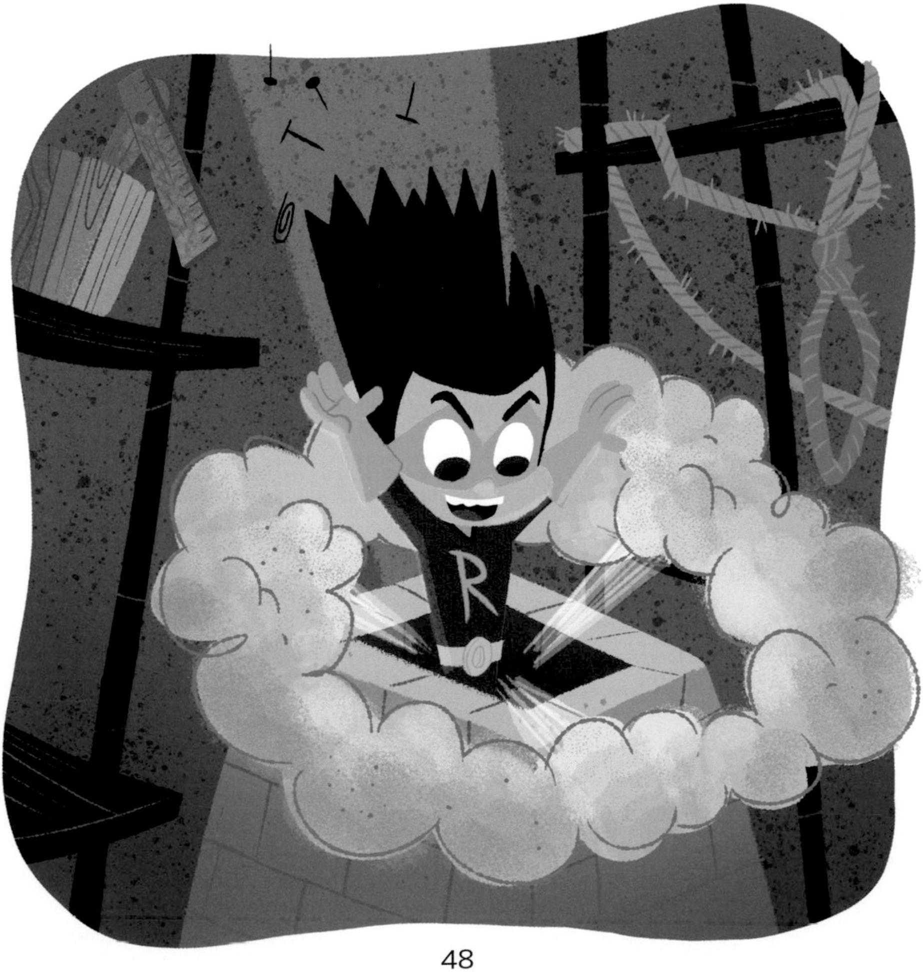
R

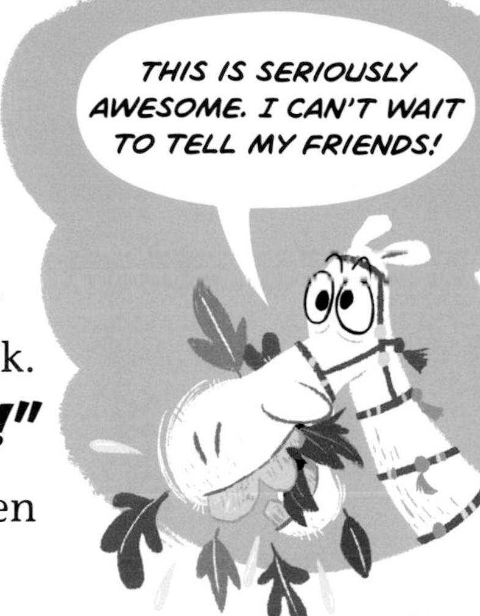
THIS IS SERIOUSLY AWESOME. I CAN'T WAIT TO TELL MY FRIENDS!

The camel landed next to the tunnel's mouth, and Drew and Ella jumped off its back.

"Thanks, camel!" Drew said. "You've been great!"

"Enjoy those wings!" Ella said.

The camel gave what looked like a smile and flew off. It **LOVED** its new wings!

"Ready?" Drew asked Ella.

"Ready!" she answered confidently.

"LET'S DO THIS!" Drew said as he jumped down into the dark tunnel with Ella right behind him!

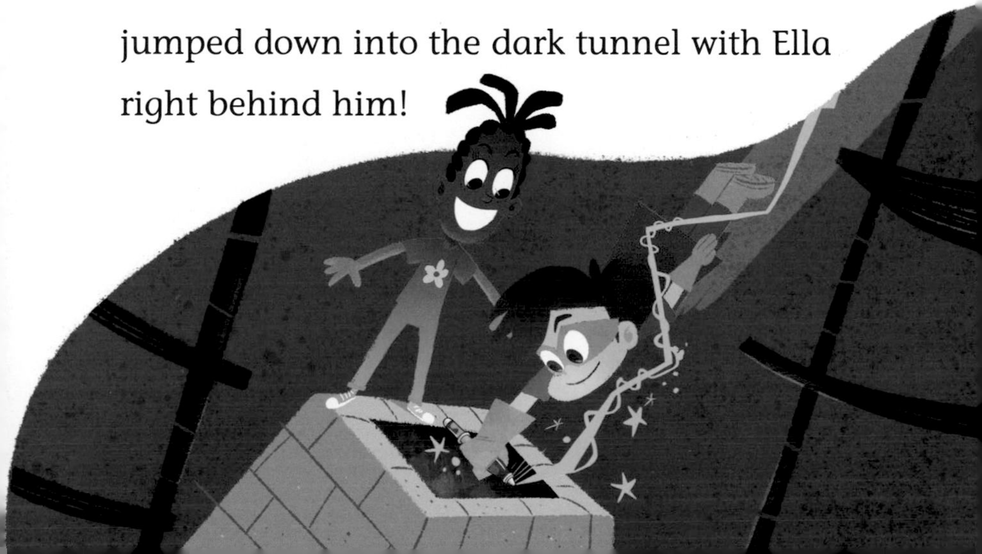

CHAPTER SIX

DREW AND ELLA made their way through the dark tunnel. It was lit only by the occasional flickering torch. In the long distances between the torches, it got **REALLY** dark!

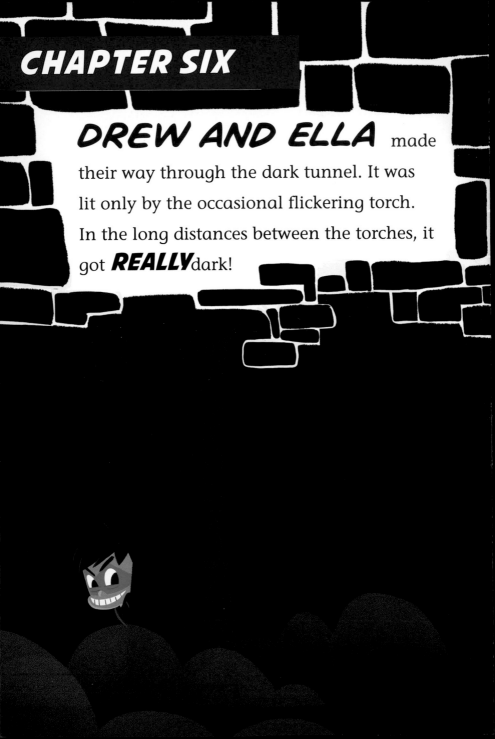

"Evil Ray!" Drew called. "Where are you? **RAY!"** But the only answer was the echo of his own voice.

"RAY ... *Ray* ... *Ray* ..."

"Where'd that evil dude go?" Ella asked.

"I don't know," Drew said, "but we've got to find him! We can't let him erase all that important stuff from history!"

So they kept walking cautiously down the long, dark tunnel, looking for Evil Ray. . . .

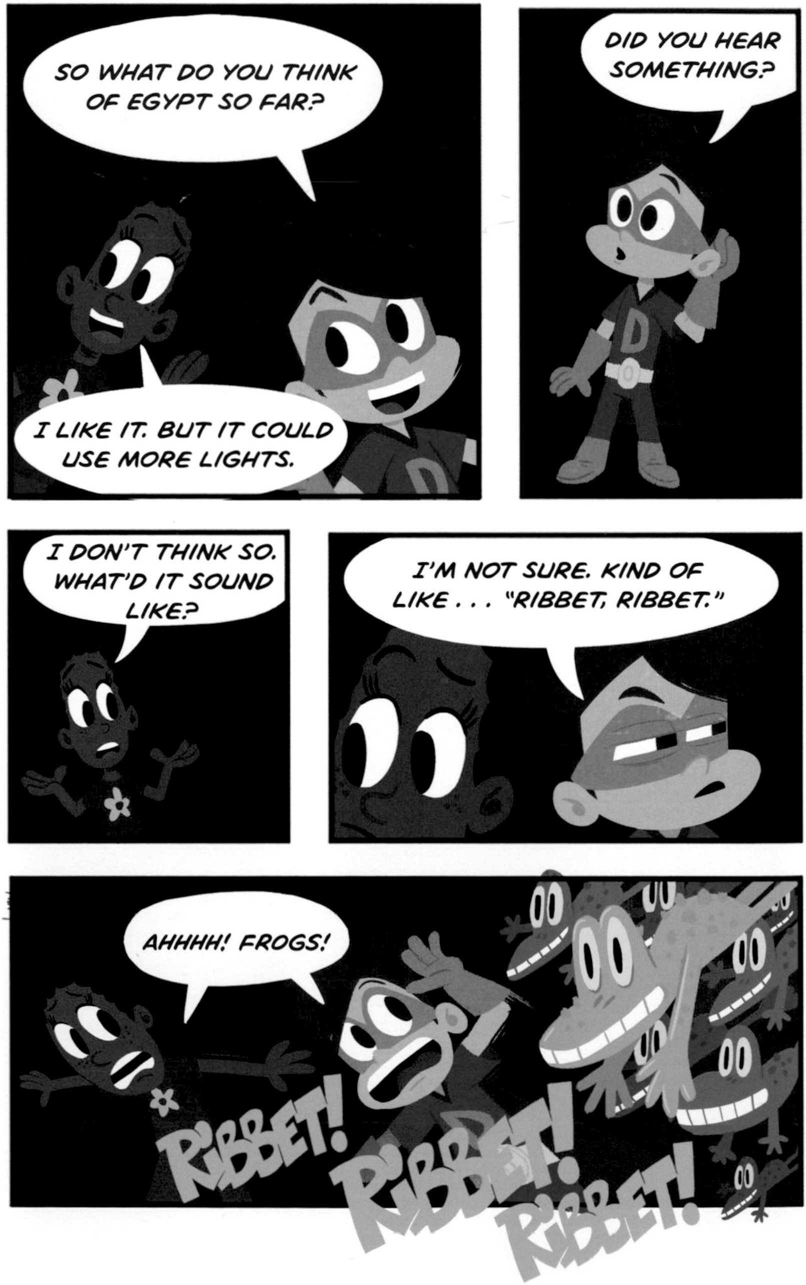
SO WHAT DO YOU THINK OF EGYPT SO FAR?
I LIKE IT. BUT IT COULD USE MORE LIGHTS.
DID YOU HEAR SOMETHING?
I DON'T THINK SO. WHAT'D IT SOUND LIKE?
I'M NOT SURE. KIND OF LIKE . . . "RIBBET, RIBBET."
AHHHH! FROGS!
RIBBET!
RIBBET!
RIBBET!

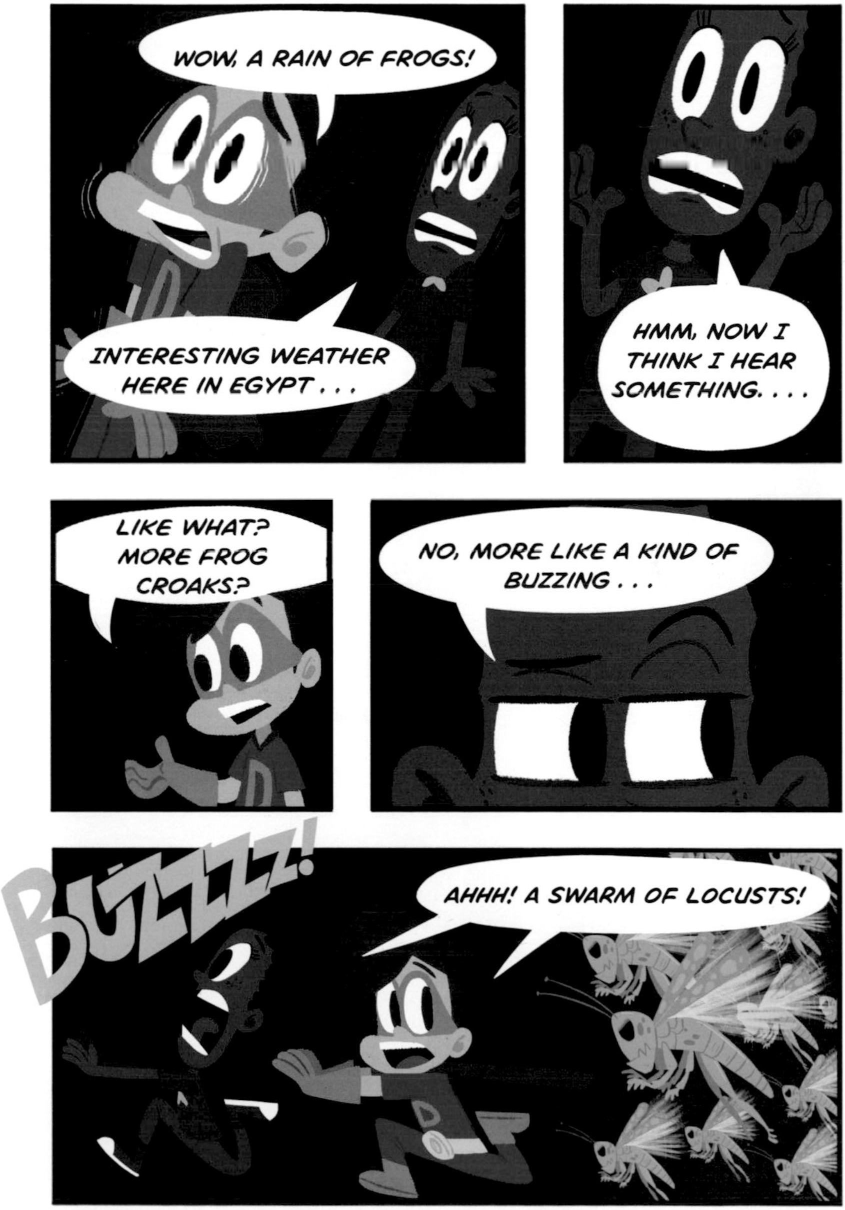
WOW, A RAIN OF FROGS!
INTERESTING WEATHER HERE IN EGYPT . . .
HMM, NOW I THINK I HEAR SOMETHING. . . .
LIKE WHAT? MORE FROG CROAKS?
NO, MORE LIKE A KIND OF BUZZING . . .
BUZZZZ!
AHHH! A SWARM OF LOCUSTS!

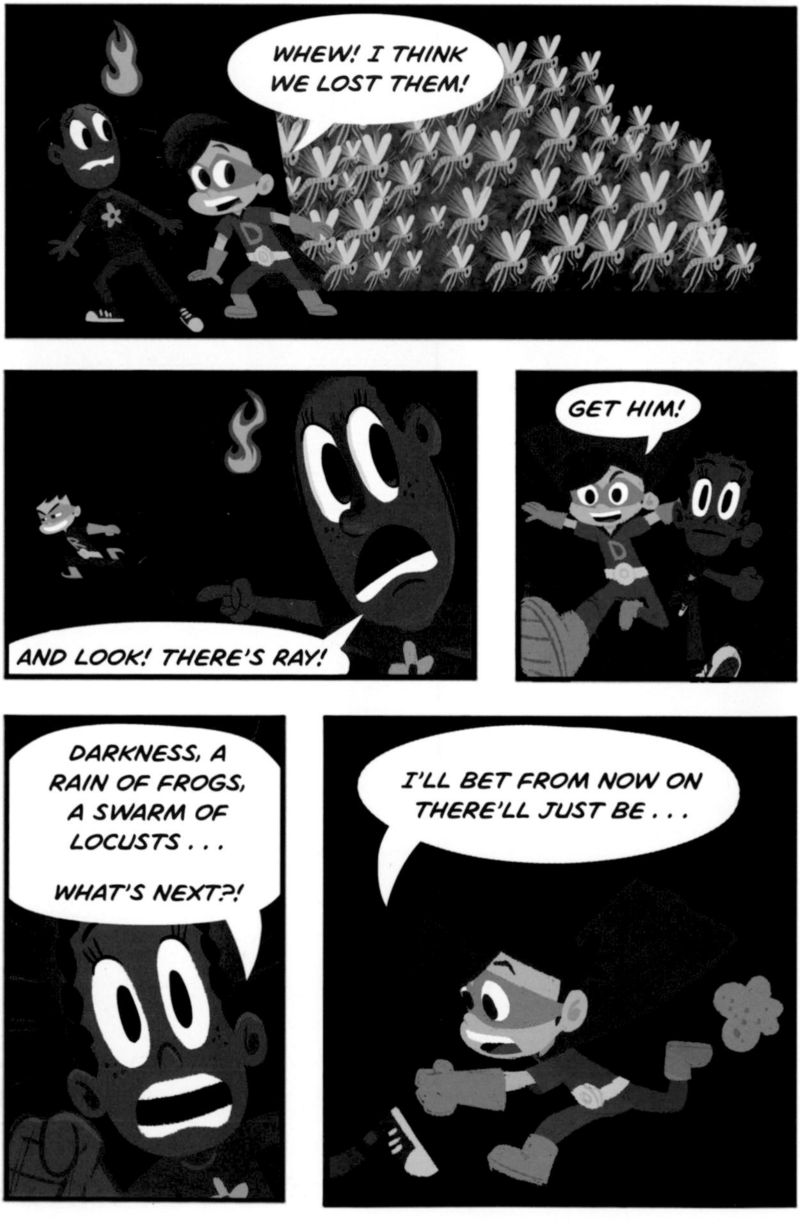
WHEW! I THINK WE LOST THEM!
AND LOOK! THERE'S RAY!
GET HIM!
DARKNESS, A RAIN OF FROGS, A SWARM OF LOCUSTS . . .
WHAT'S NEXT?!
I'LL BET FROM NOW ON THERE'LL JUST BE . . .

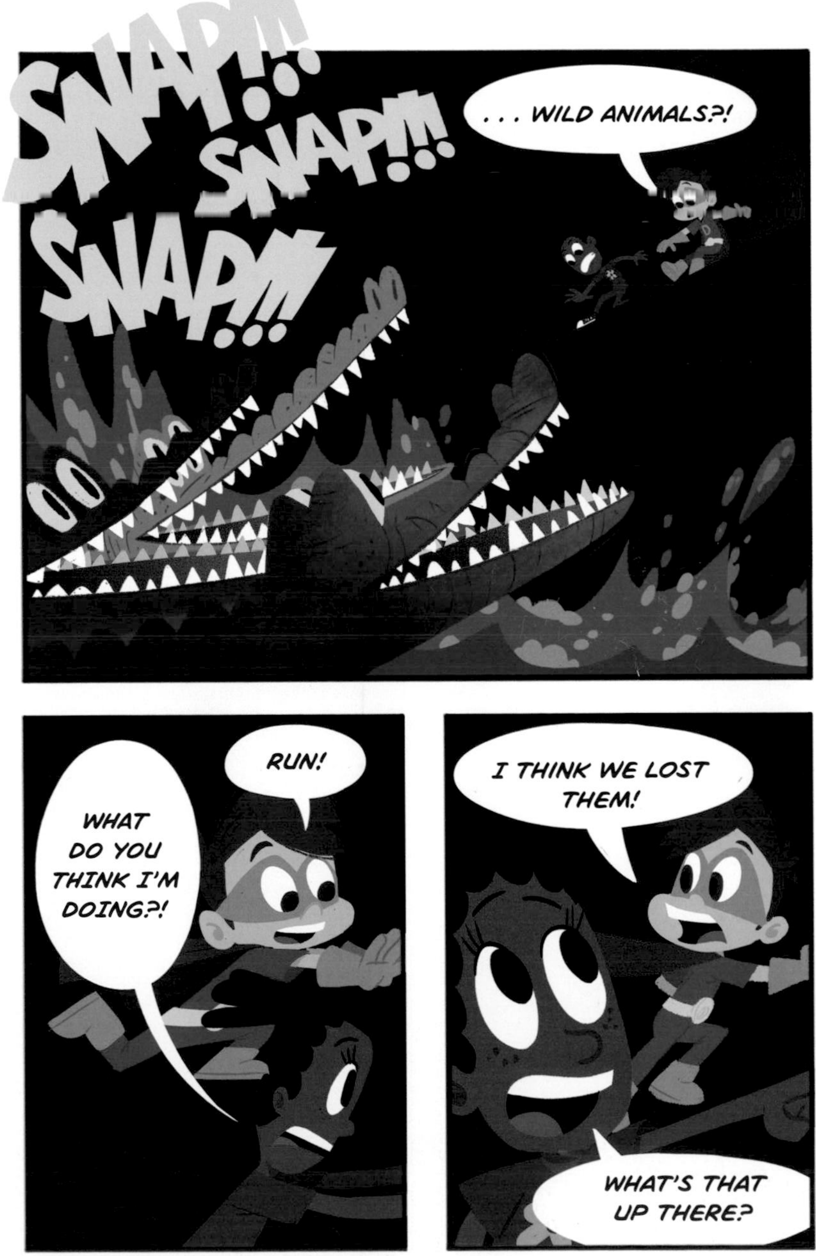
SNAP!!!
SNAP!!!
SNAP!!!
. . . WILD ANIMALS?!
RUN!
WHAT DO YOU THINK I'M DOING?!
I THINK WE LOST THEM!
WHAT'S THAT UP THERE?

They crept forward **cautiously.** When they got closer, they could see that what Ella spotted looked a bit like **a big wooden trunk** standing on one end. Only . . . it was shaped like a **person.** And it had a **face** and arms carved on it!

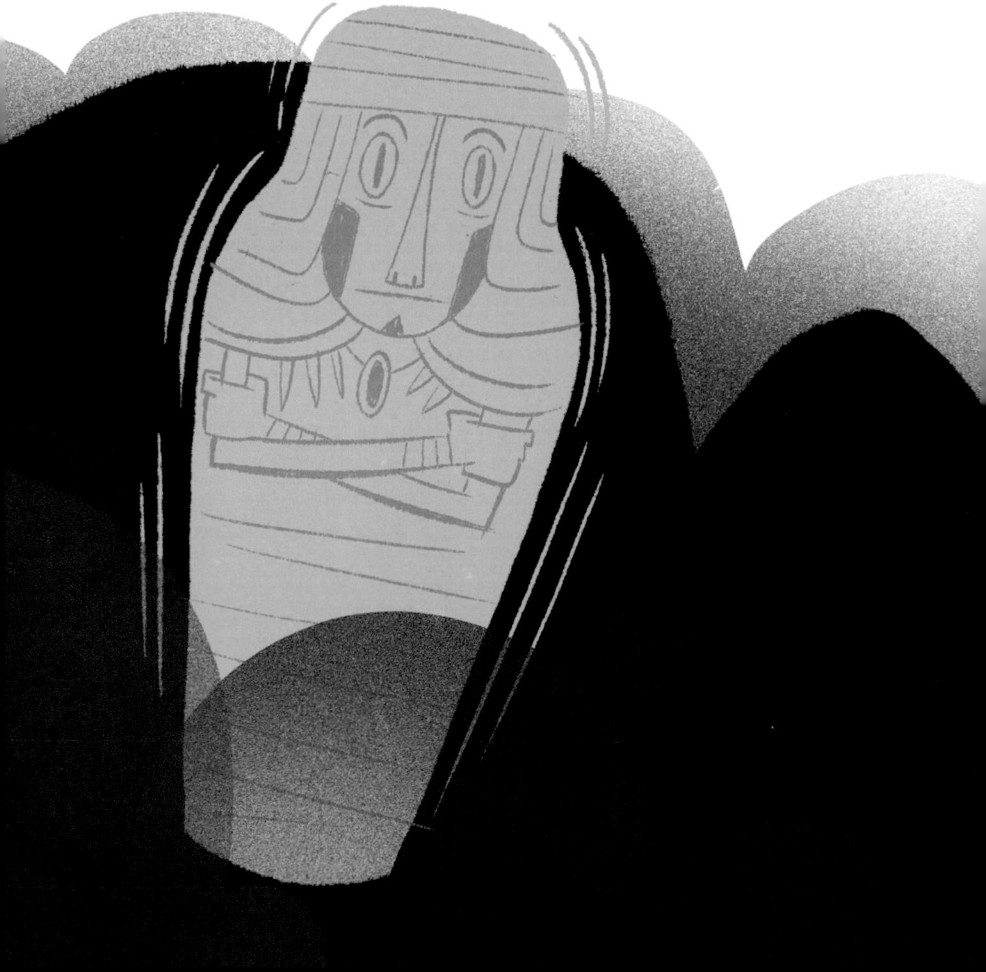

"It looks like some kind of **container,"** Ella said. "I wonder what's inside?"

"It looks like a giant ***mummy case*** to me!" Drew said.

BUMP! BUMP! BUMP!

The mummy case started rocking back and forth!

CHAPTER SEVEN

"UM, I THINK IT'S ALIVE!" Ella said, sounding a little scared. "Or at least something inside there is alive!"

"BOO!"

"AHHHHHHH!"

Drew and Ella screamed.

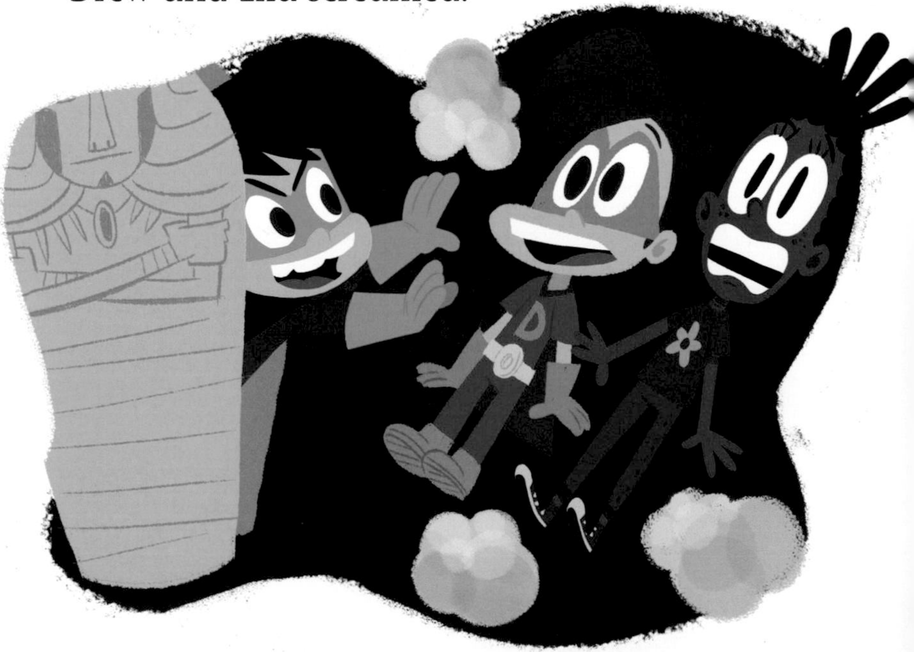

"Ha ha ha!" Ray laughed. He'd jumped out from the darkness and booed them! "What's the matter, fraidy-cats? Scared of your mummy?!"

Drew *had* been startled by Ray jumping out and yelling "boo," but he wasn't about to admit that to his evil twin. "Hand over that ***Magic Eraser, Evil Ray!***"

"No way!" Ray cackled. "In fact, I'm going to use my Magic Eraser to erase your ***time machine***. You'll be stuck in ancient Egypt ***FOREVER!***"

Now Drew thought ancient Egypt was a very interesting place to visit. But he didn't want to be stuck there **FOREVER**. Drew and Ella **REALLY** had to stop Ray!

"I said **GIVE ME THAT ERASER!"** Drew repeated. He lunged at Ray, trying to snatch the Magic Eraser out of his hands, but Ray darted away into the darkness. They ran all around the dark chamber where they'd found the giant mummy case. The case kept rocking back and forth.

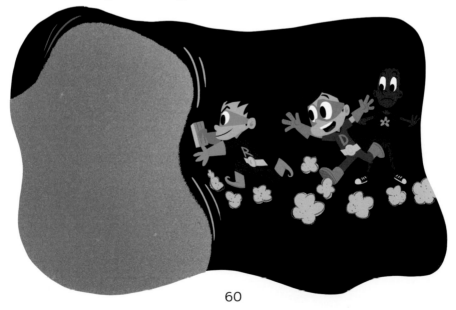

BUMP! BUMP! BUMP! BUMP!

Every time Drew thought he'd caught up with Ray, his evil twin ducked and dodged, slipping away. Finally Drew jumped forward, taking the chance that he'd be able to tackle Ray in the dark.

It worked! Drew held onto Ray as they rolled across the floor, not letting him get away. "Let go of me!" Ray yelled.

"No!" Drew said. "Not until you give me that Magic Eraser!"

"Don't forget," Ray threatened. "The Magic Eraser works on **YOU, TOO!**" He started to move the eraser toward Drew to erase the superhero!

"You'll never erase me!" Drew said. Ella had to do **SOMETHING.**

BUMP! BUMP! BUMP!

The mummy case! It was still rocking back and forth!

Ella knew what to do. She ran over to the big case and opened it.

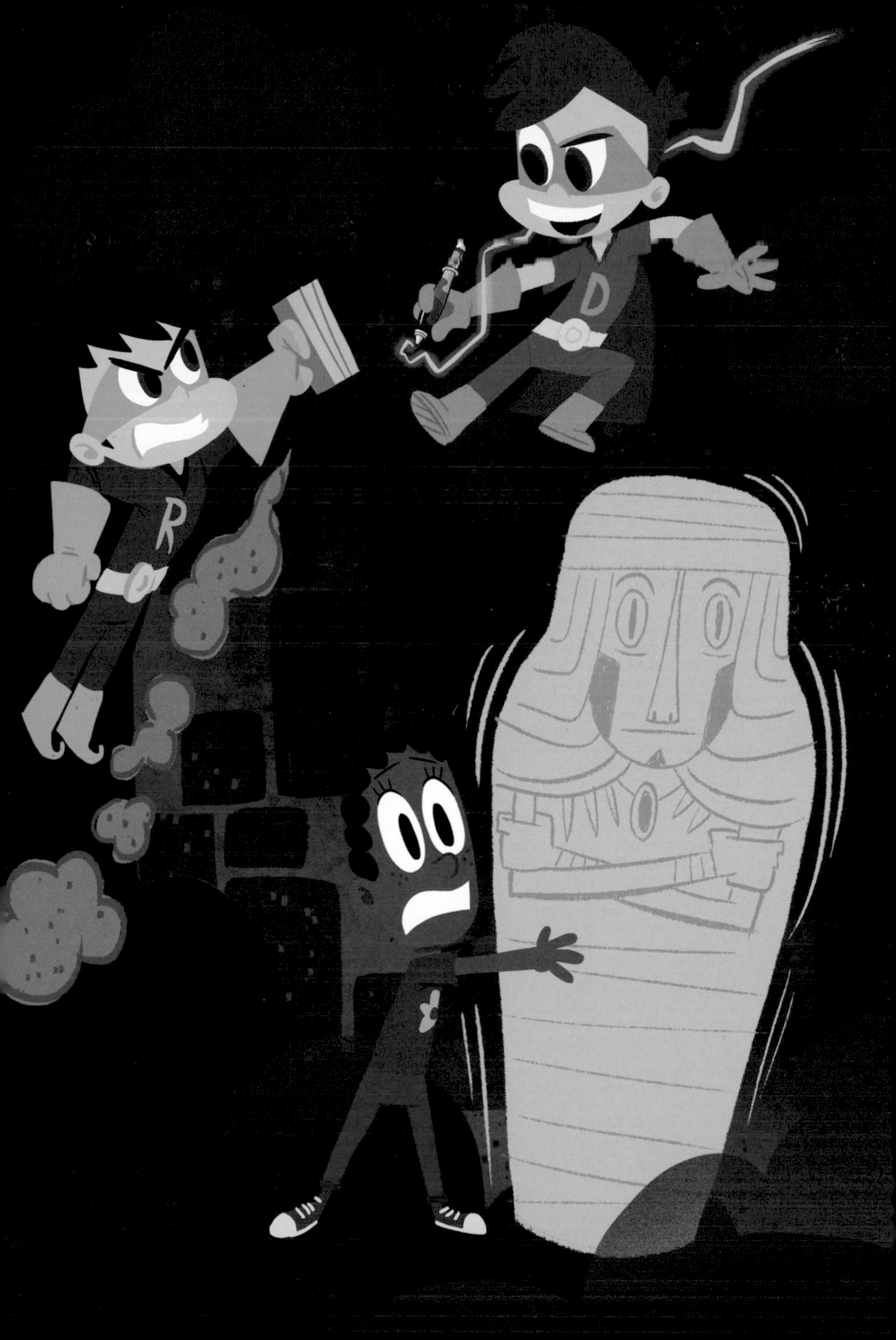

CHAPTER EIGHT

INSIDE THE MUMMY CASE

was . . . ***A MUMMY!*** Wrapped all in bandages, it lifted its arms and stepped out of the case, groaning.

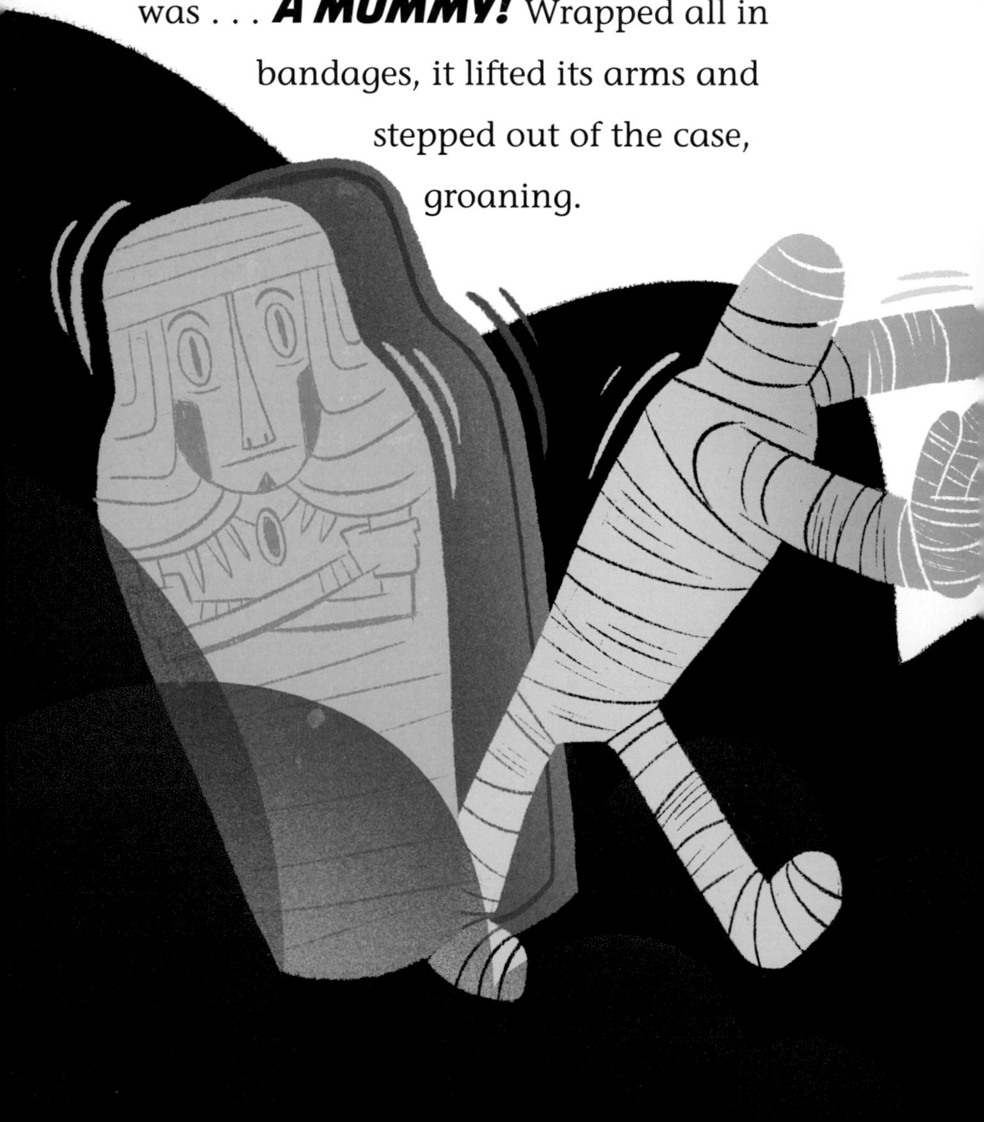

"NNUNNH! NUNNNHHH!"

Ella ducked behind the open case so the mummy wouldn't see her. Instead, it went straight toward Drew and Ray!

Drew and Ray turned and saw the mummy staggering toward them.

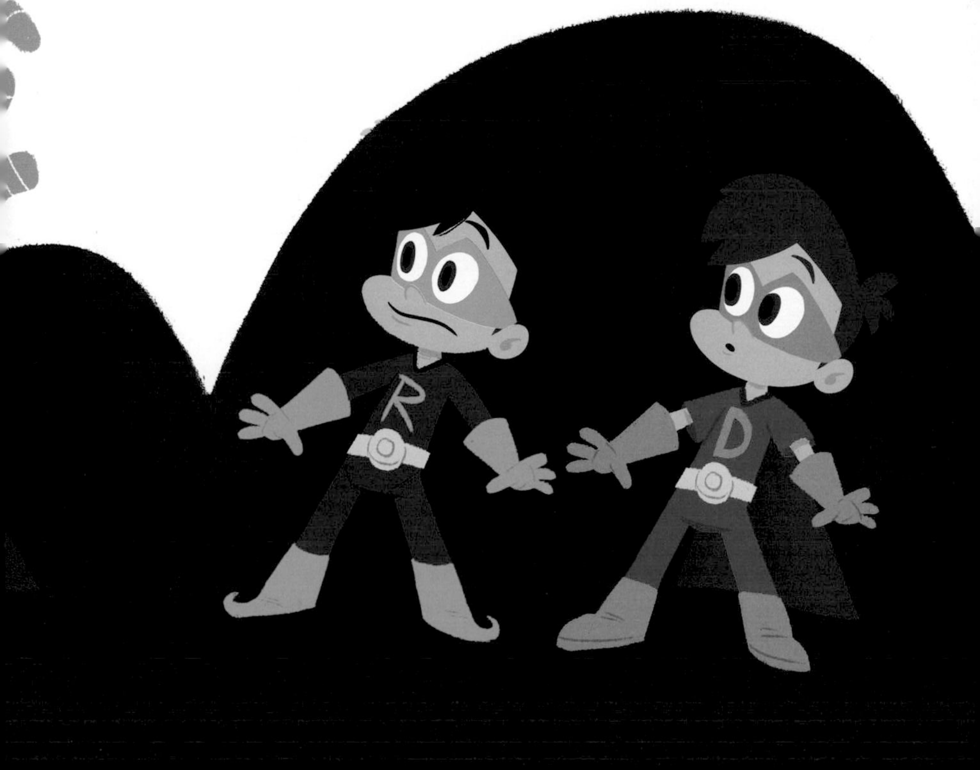

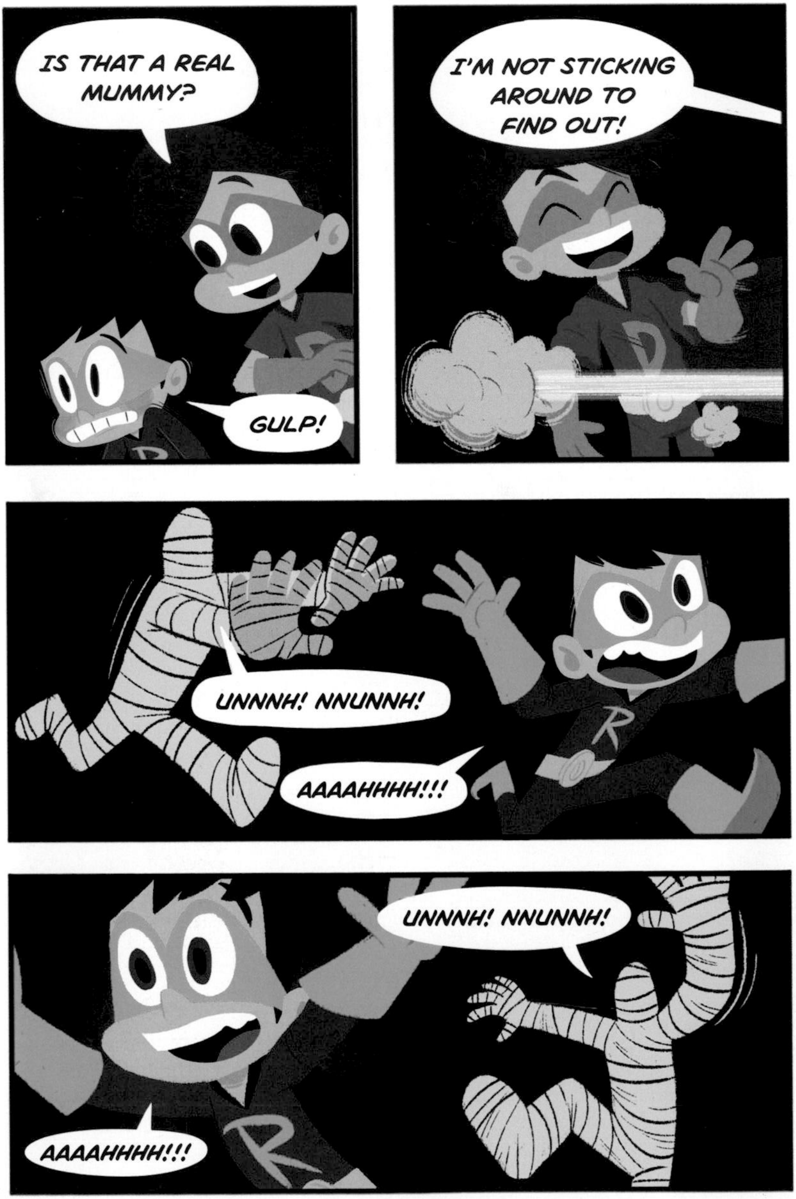
IS THAT A REAL MUMMY?
GULP!
I'M NOT STICKING AROUND TO FIND OUT!
UNNNH! NNUNNH!
AAAAHHHH!!!
UNNNH! NNUNNH!
AAAAHHHH!!!

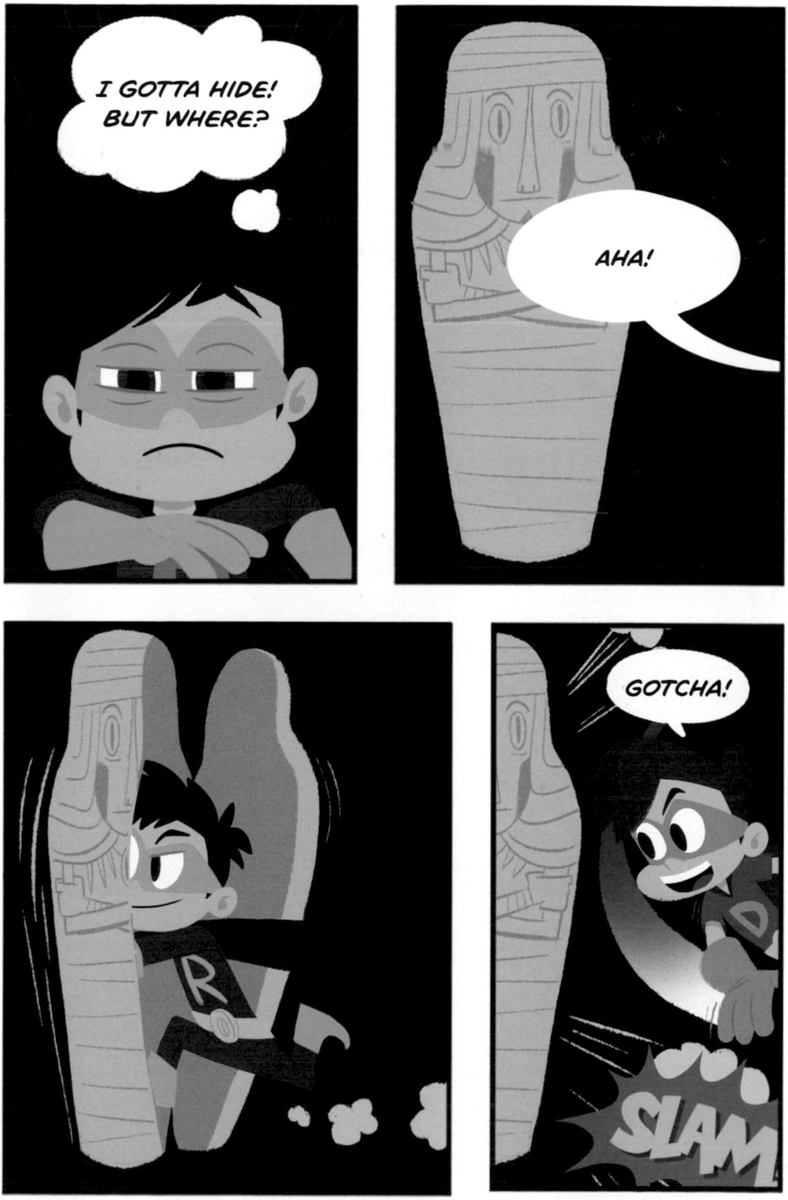
I GOTTA HIDE! BUT WHERE?
AHA!
GOTCHA!
SLAM

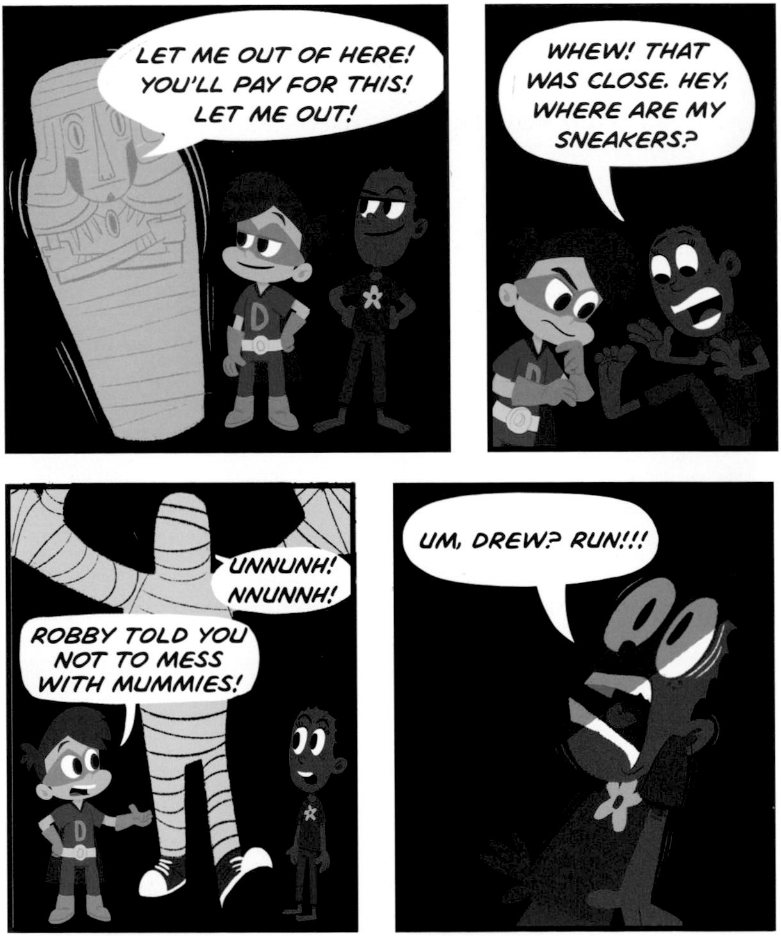
LET ME OUT OF HERE! YOU'LL PAY FOR THIS! LET ME OUT!
WHEW! THAT WAS CLOSE. HEY, WHERE ARE MY SNEAKERS?
UNNUNH! NNUNNH!
ROBBY TOLD YOU NOT TO MESS WITH MUMMIES!
UM, DREW? RUN!!!

The mummy chased Drew and Ella all through the dark tunnels! After a while, they were pretty sure they were just running around in circles.

"I think I've seen that torch before," Ella said as they ran past a lit torch.

"We've got to get out of here!" Drew said.

"NNNUNH! UNNNH!" the mummy groaned as it ran after them.

"I've got an idea!" Drew said as they ran.

"What is it?" Ella said. "Spend the rest of our lives in these tunnels? 'Cause if that's your idea, I'm against it!"

"No," Drew said. "That's not it. We're underground, right?"

"Right," Ella agreed.

"So I figure we need to go **UP!**" Drew said.

"I agree," Ella said, "but how? We haven't found any stairways."

"Leave that to me!" Drew said, taking out his **Mighty Pen Ultimate. . . .**

CHAPTER NINE

DREW QUICKLY sketched a super-cool elevator platform powered by jet rockets. It was square, with a jet rocket at each corner. "There!" he said proudly. "One elevator, going up!"

"Perfect!" Ella said, clapping her hands. "We'd better jump on it, because here comes the mummy!"

"NNUNN! NUNNNHHH!" moaned the mummy as it staggered down the dark tunnel toward them.

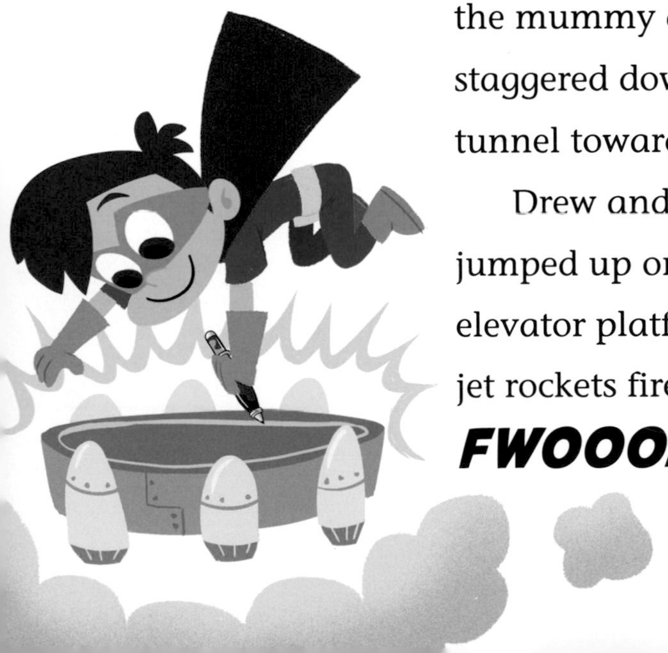

Drew and Ella jumped up on the elevator platform. The jet rockets fired up!

FWOOOM!

The platform lifted up off the ground just as the mummy arrived. He tried to grab the platform, but it was just out of his reach. **"AWWWGH!"** he groaned. Then he turned around and stomped back down the shadowy hall.

"Enjoy my shoes!" Ella called after him.

The elevator platform lifted the two time travelers through a tunnel that ran up and down like a giant chimney. As they rose, they saw the blue sky high above them. The little blue square of sky at the top of the tunnel got bigger and bigger as they got closer to it. A second later they were out of the tunnel, flying through the air!

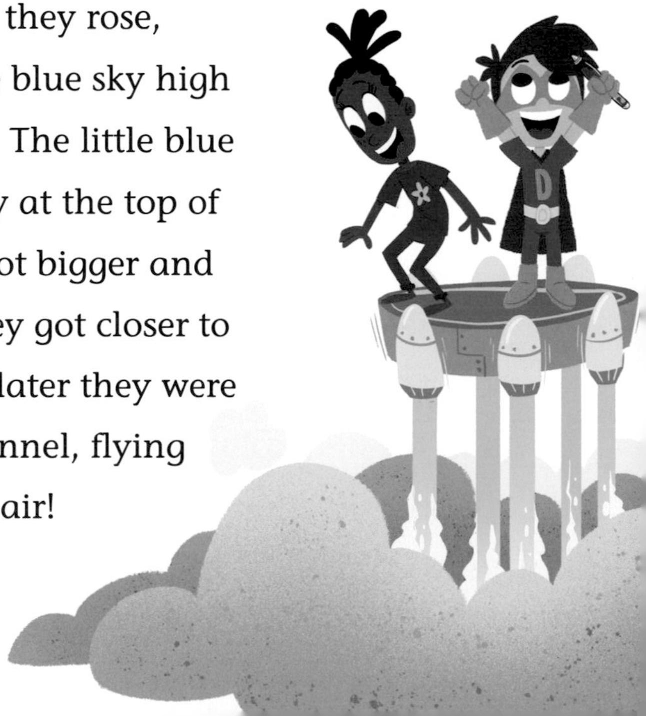

"Boy, am I glad to be out of that dark old place!" Ella said.

"Me, too!" Drew agreed.

The elevator flew them up to the top of the Great Sphinx. As they passed the Sphinx's face, Drew got an idea. "Elevator, **PAUSE!"**

The elevator hovered in the air, right in front of the spot where the Sphinx's nose had been before Ray erased it.

"Your elevator has voice commands?" Ella asked, impressed.

"Of course!" Drew said. "That's the way I drew it! Now to draw something else. . . ."

He pulled out his trusty **Pen Ultimate** and quickly sketched a new nose for the Sphinx! It was a little bigger than the original nose, but at least now the Sphinx wasn't nose-less.

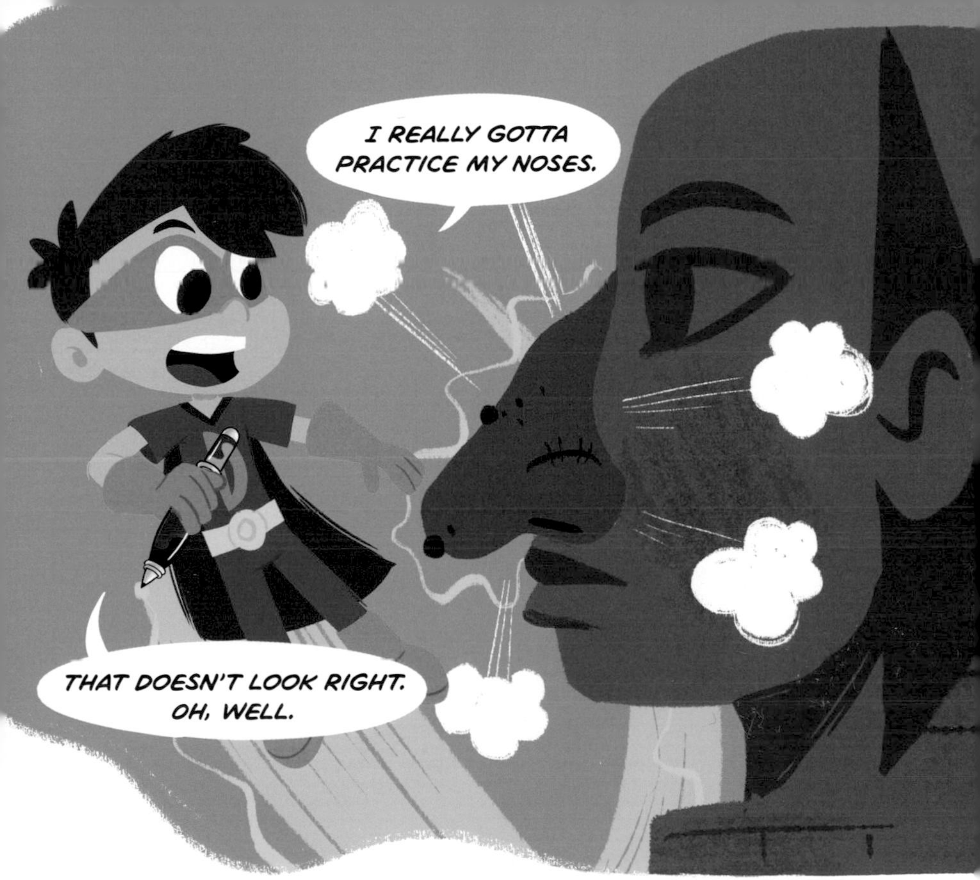
I REALLY GOTTA PRACTICE MY NOSES.
THAT DOESN'T LOOK RIGHT. OH, WELL.

Drew told the elevator to take them back to their time machine, and that's exactly what it did. Waving goodbye to the Egyptian boy and girl, Drew and Ella hopped back into the time machine and closed the door.

The boy and girl were amazed when the time machine started to glow and shake. And then . . . **POOF!** It disappeared!

Then they looked up at the sky and saw a camel happily flying overhead. The boy and girl looked at each other and shrugged. Kooky things happen in Egypt!

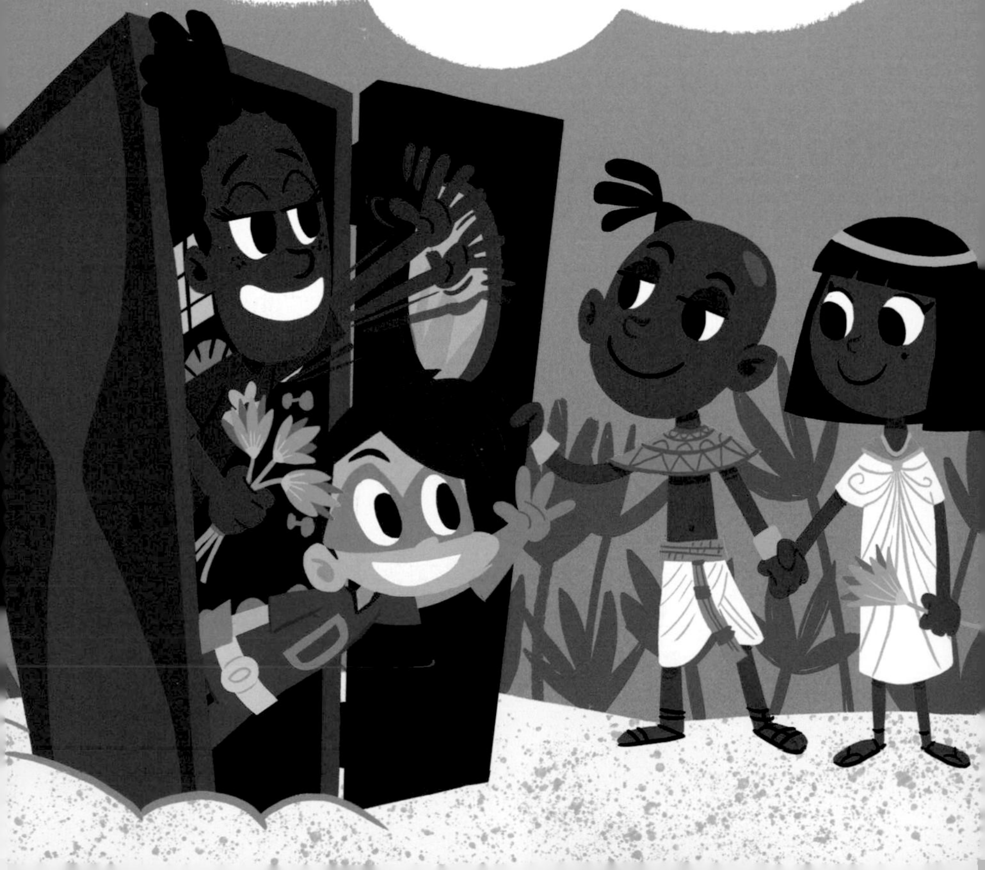

CHAPTER TEN

INSIDE the time machine, Drew had set the dial for the present day. After a lot of shaking and vibrating, the time machine came to a stop.

"Are we here? I mean, there? I mean, back where we started, at the museum?" Ella asked.

"There's only one way to find out," Drew said. He unbuckled his seat belt, stood up, opened the door . . .

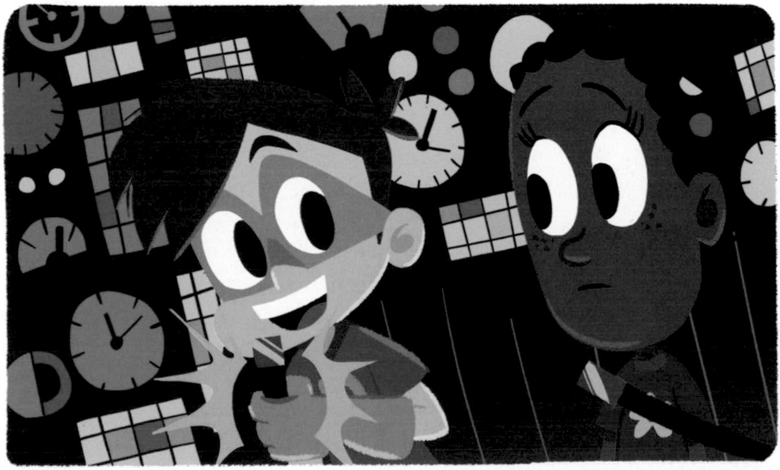

. . . and saw that they were right back in the museum, where they had started their adventure. When they stepped out of the time machine, they were in the museum's Hall of Ancient Egypt. They looked through the door to the big glass-walled room that held the Great Sphinx replica . . . and the Sphinx had the goofy nose Drew had drawn!

They ran toward the Great Sphinx exhibit to admire the nose. Nikki and Robby turned around and saw Drew and Ella hurrying into the hall.  **"Where have you two been?"** Nikki asked.

"Yeah, you missed all the ***cool stuff*** we learned about Egypt!" Robby said.

Drew and Ella looked at each other and smiled.

"You mean stuff like that sometimes camels can fly?" Ella said.

"Or that frogs can fall down from the sky like rain?" Drew asked.

"Or that mummies can come out of their cases and chase you through dark, creepy tunnels?" Ella asked.

"And steal your shoes?" Drew added, laughing.

"What are you two **TALKING** about?" Nikki asked. "We learned that pharaohs were the kings of Egypt."

"Oh, that's interesting, too," Ella said, smiling.

Robby looked down at Ella's bare feet. "By the way, Ella," he said, "where are your purple sneakers? Did you lose them?"

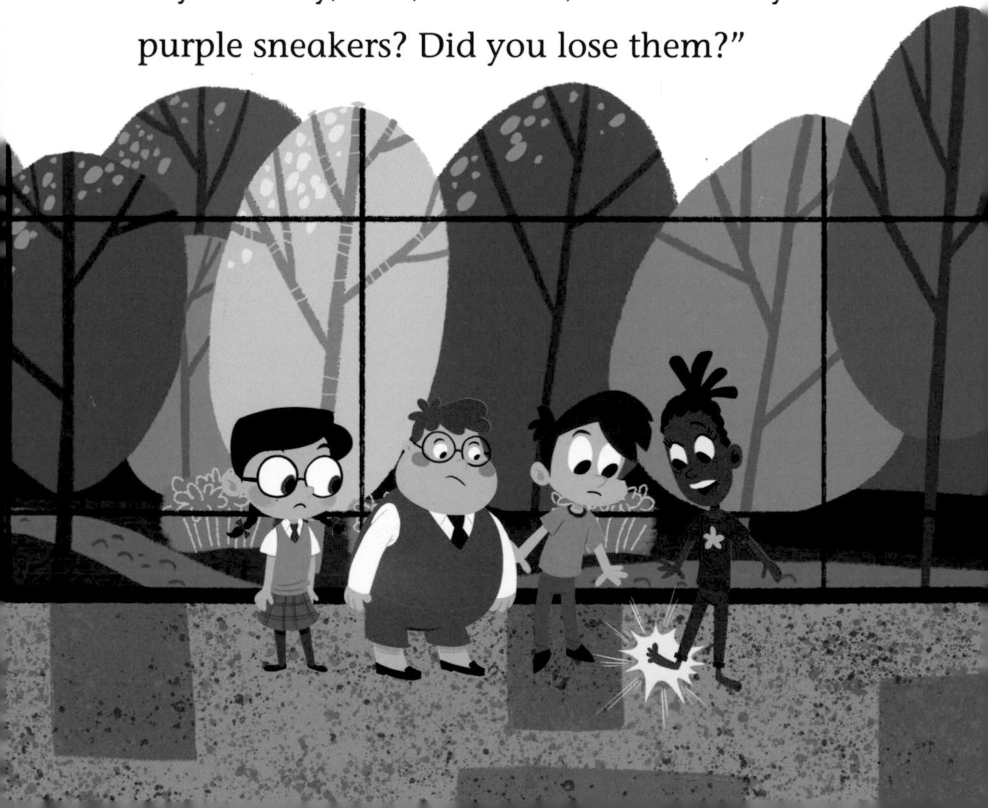

Ella looked at Drew. **"Ask my mummy,"** she said. Then she and Drew both burst out laughing.

Robby and Nikki just looked at each other, not understanding what was so funny.

Crafty Carol leaned in through the door from the next gallery. **"Come on, kids!"** she called. "There's much, much more to see and enjoy here in the museum! This field trip is just getting started!" Then she noticed the big nose on the Sphinx. "Hm," she said. "I never noticed how big the Sphinx's nose is before!"

As they followed Crafty Carol into the next gallery, Ella and Drew hung back a little, talking. . . .

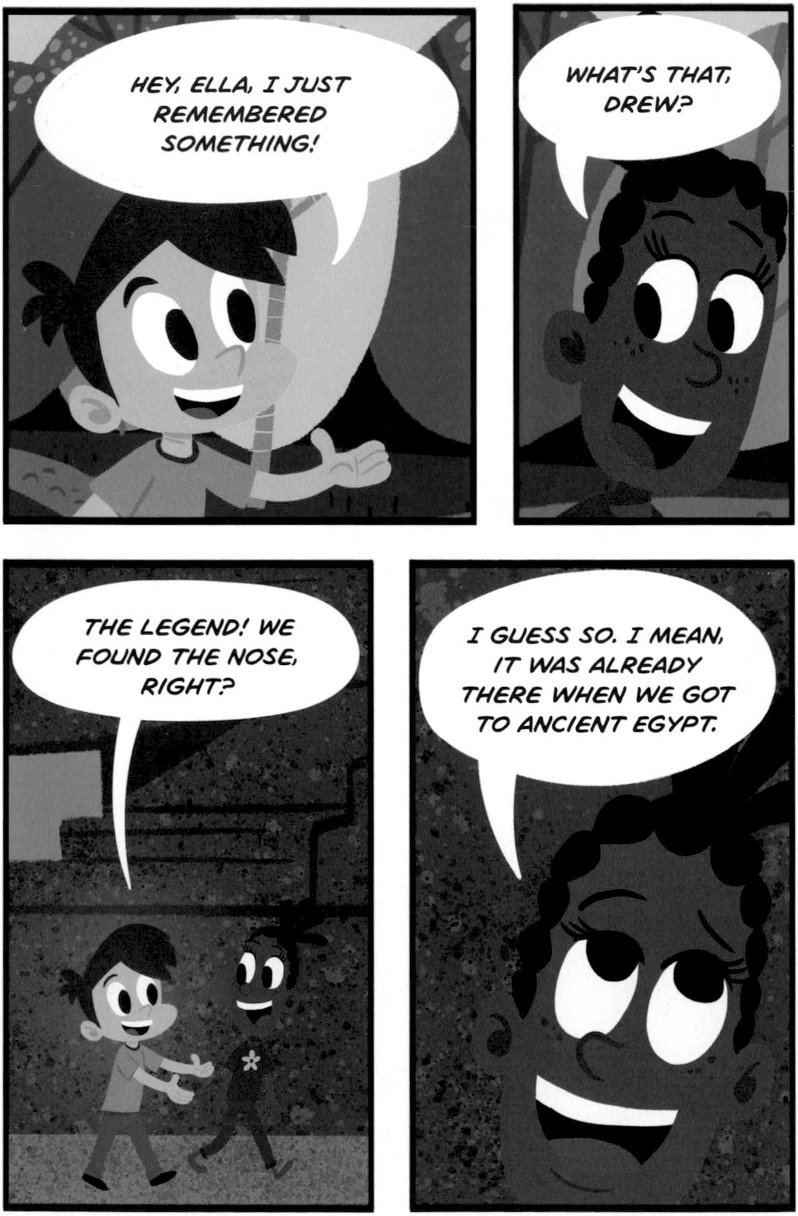
HEY, ELLA, I JUST REMEMBERED SOMETHING!
WHAT'S THAT, DREW?
THE LEGEND! WE FOUND THE NOSE, RIGHT?
I GUESS SO. I MEAN, IT WAS ALREADY THERE WHEN WE GOT TO ANCIENT EGYPT.

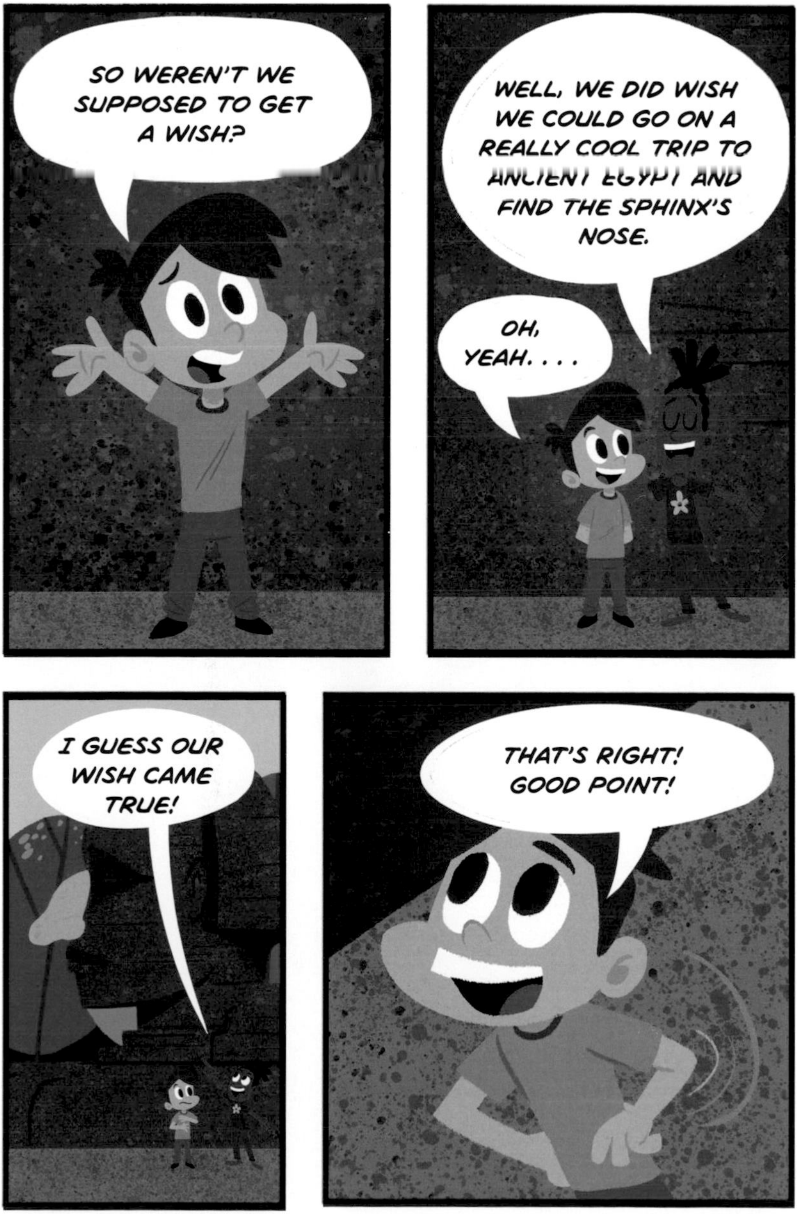
SO WEREN'T WE SUPPOSED TO GET A WISH?
WELL, WE DID WISH WE COULD GO ON A REALLY COOL TRIP TO ANCIENT EGYPT AND FIND THE SPHINX'S NOSE.
OH, YEAH. . . .
I GUESS OUR WISH CAME TRUE!
THAT'S RIGHT! GOOD POINT!

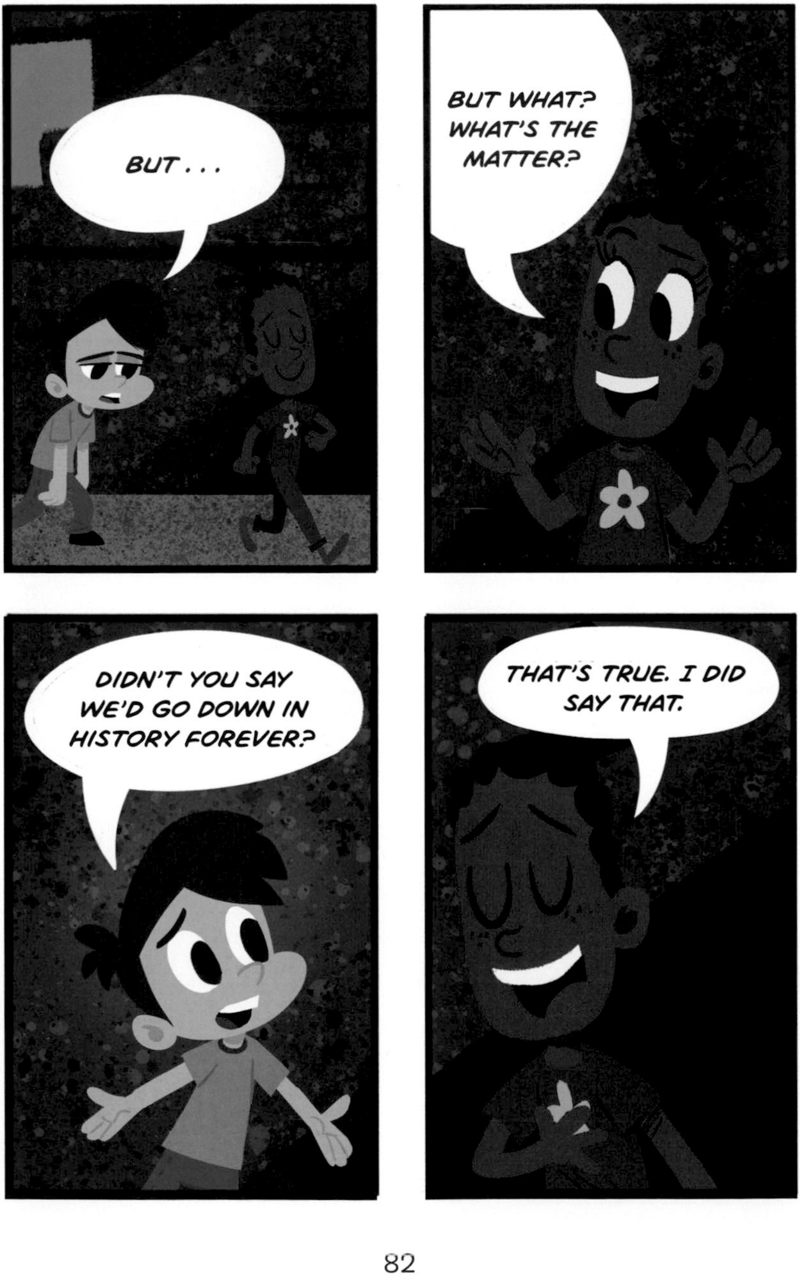
BUT . . .
BUT WHAT? WHAT'S THE MATTER?
DIDN'T YOU SAY WE'D GO DOWN IN HISTORY FOREVER?
THAT'S TRUE. I DID SAY THAT.

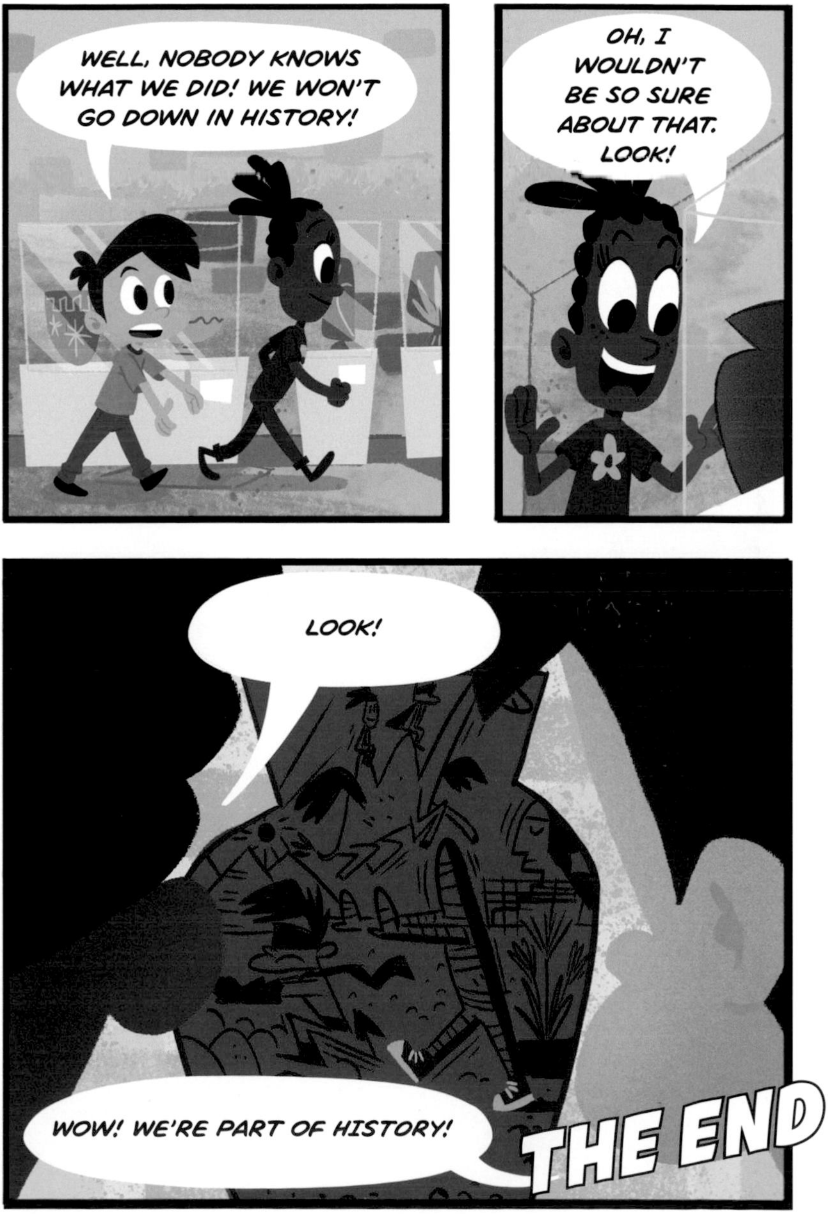
WELL, NOBODY KNOWS WHAT WE DID! WE WON'T GO DOWN IN HISTORY!
OH, I WOULDN'T BE SO SURE ABOUT THAT. LOOK!
LOOK!
WOW! WE'RE PART OF HISTORY!
THE END

DO YOU LIKE

amazing stories filled with awesome adventures?

Would you like to read about the coolest summer camp ever?

Does working together as a team to overcome an evil plan sound exciting?

Then turn the page for:

COOL SCHOOL
DREW PENDOUS
and the Camp Color War

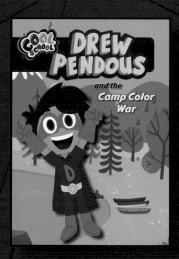

Ah, good ol' summertime! When Drew and all his friends from Cool School went to . . .

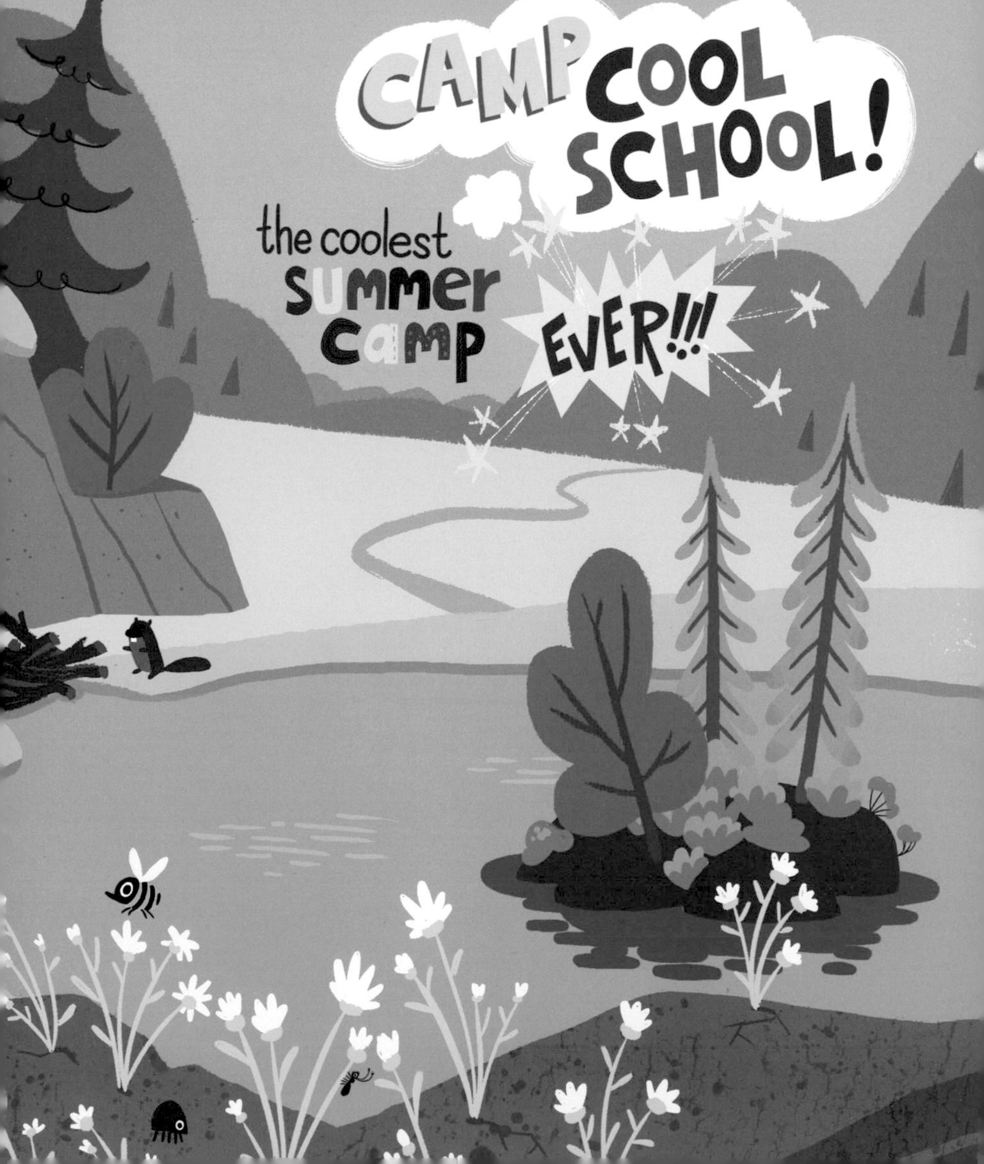
CAMP COOL SCHOOL!
the coolest summer camp
EVER!!!

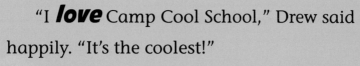

"I **love** Camp Cool School," Drew said happily. "It's the coolest!"

Camp Cool School was up in the mountains next to a clear, blue lake. All around the camp were shady woods.

"There are a **ton** of fun things to do at Camp Cool School," Drew said.

He was right.

You could

swim

in the lake.

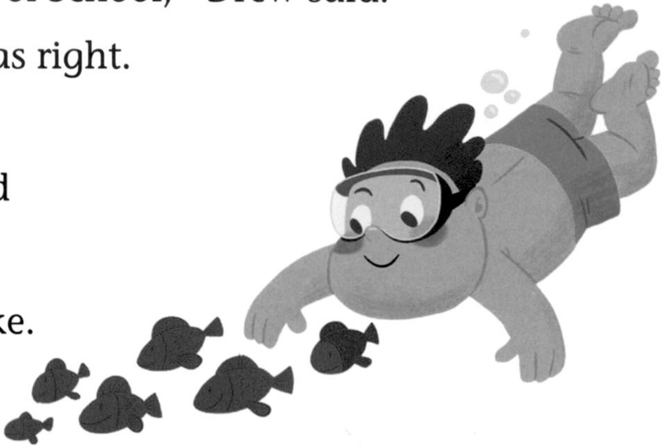

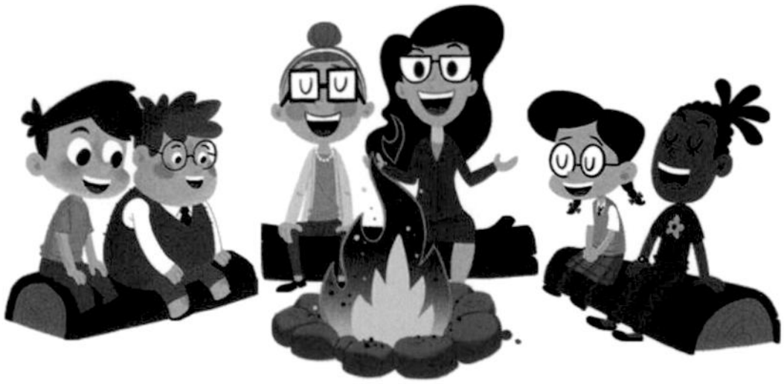

You could ***sing songs*** around a campfire.

You could go for a ***hike***.

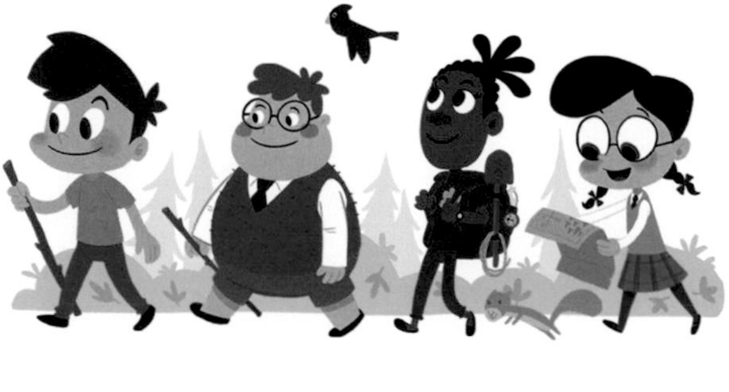

You could ***paddle a canoe*** or a kayak.

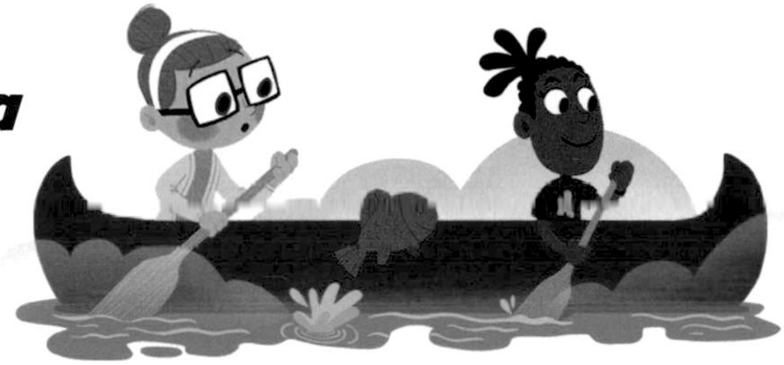

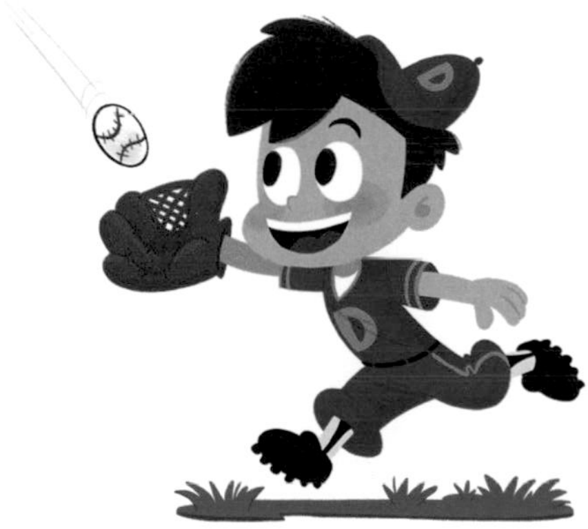

You could play ***baseball*** or ***soccer***.

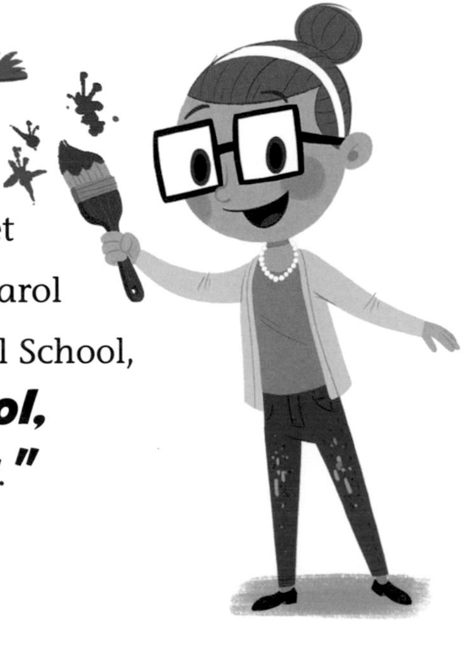

"And don't forget the crafts!" Crafty Carol said. "At Camp Cool School, we make lots of ***cool, woodsy crafts***."

At Camp Cool School, Drew's teachers were the camp counselors. Let's see. . . . Who else was at Camp Cool School that summer?

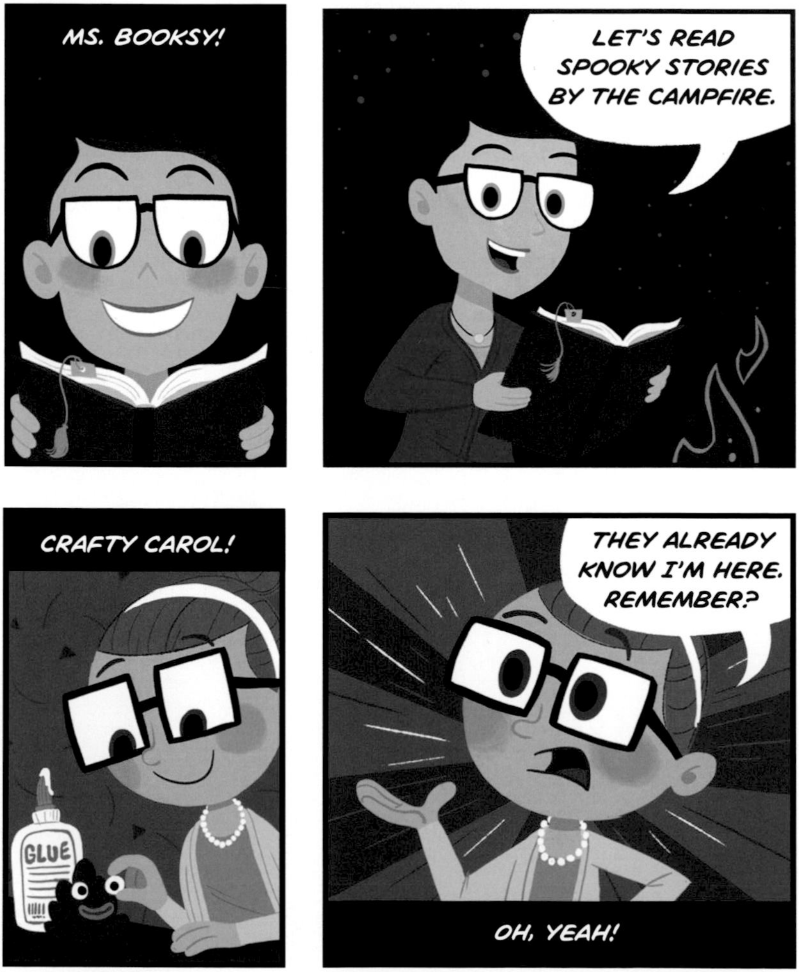
MS. BOOKSY!
LET'S READ SPOOKY STORIES BY THE CAMPFIRE.
CRAFTY CAROL!
GLUE
THEY ALREADY KNOW I'M HERE. REMEMBER?
OH, YEAH!

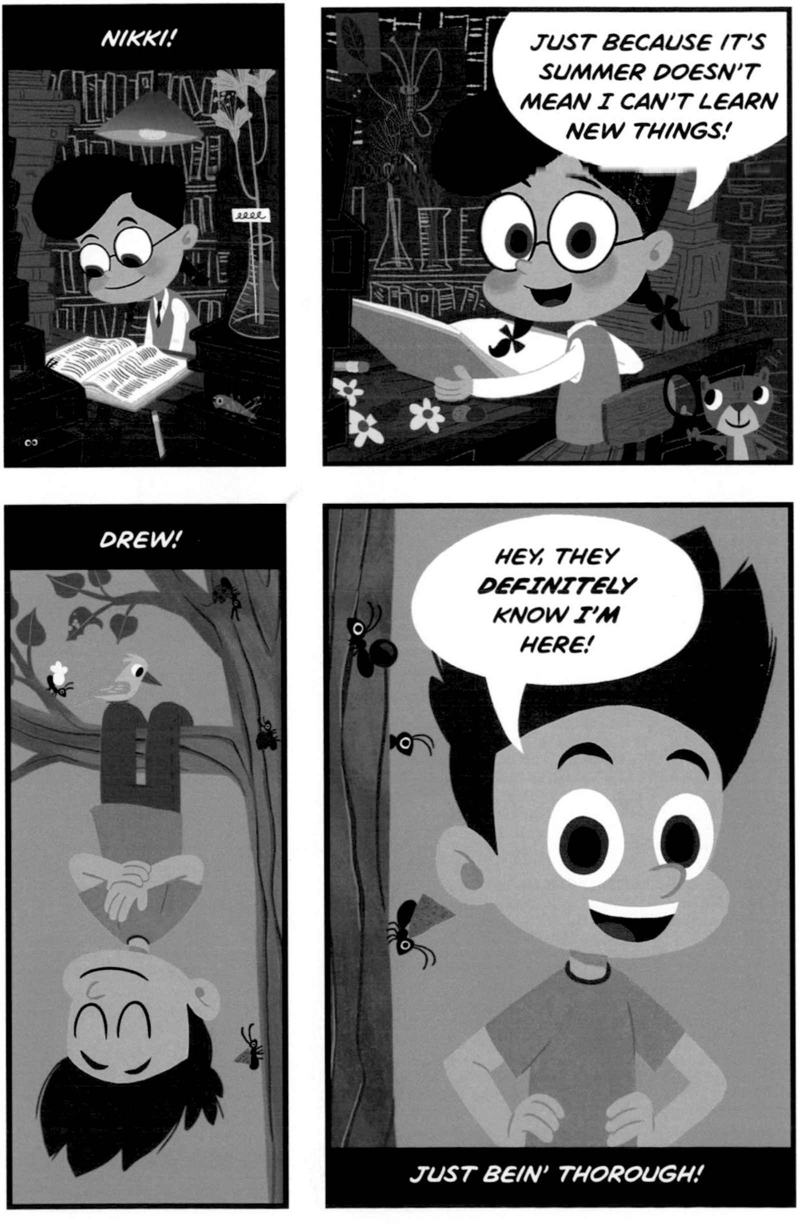
NIKKI!
JUST BECAUSE IT'S SUMMER DOESN'T MEAN I CAN'T LEARN NEW THINGS!
DREW!
HEY, THEY DEFINITELY KNOW I'M HERE!
JUST BEIN' THOROUGH!

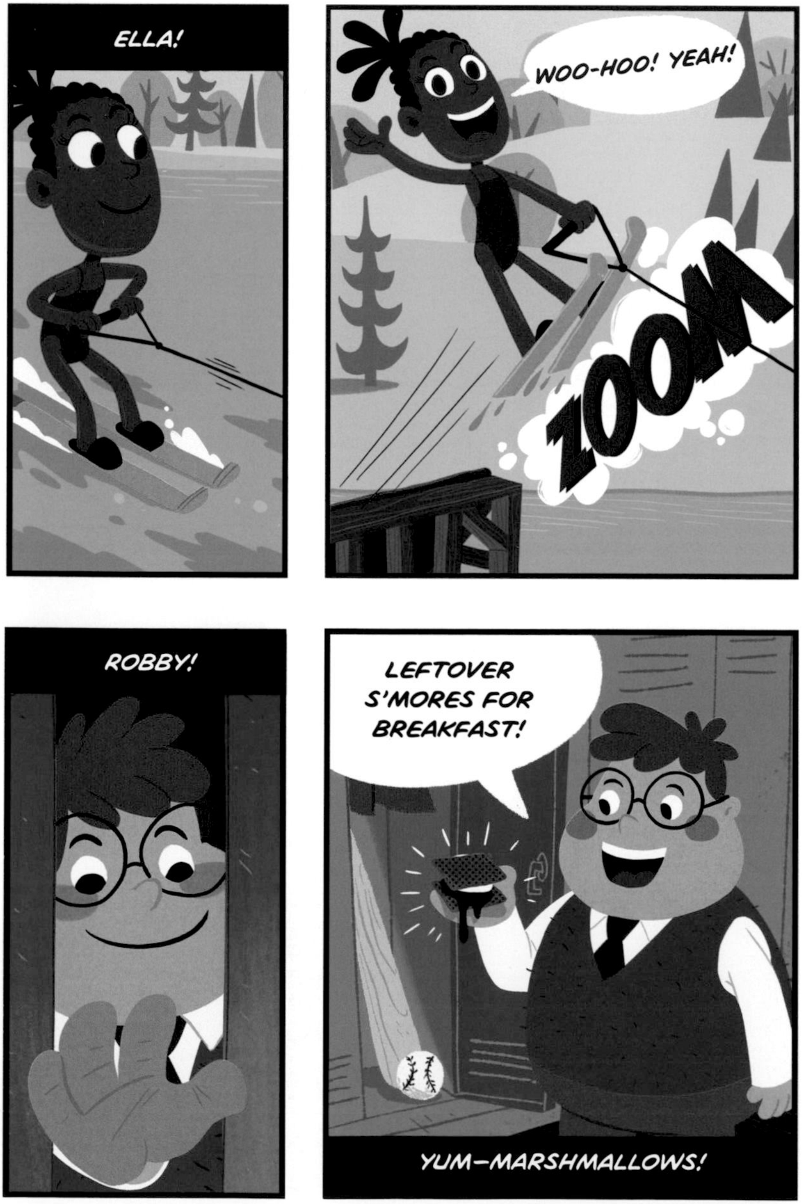
ELLA!
WOO-HOO! YEAH!
ZOOM
ROBBY!
LEFTOVER S'MORES FOR BREAKFAST!
YUM—MARSHMALLOWS!

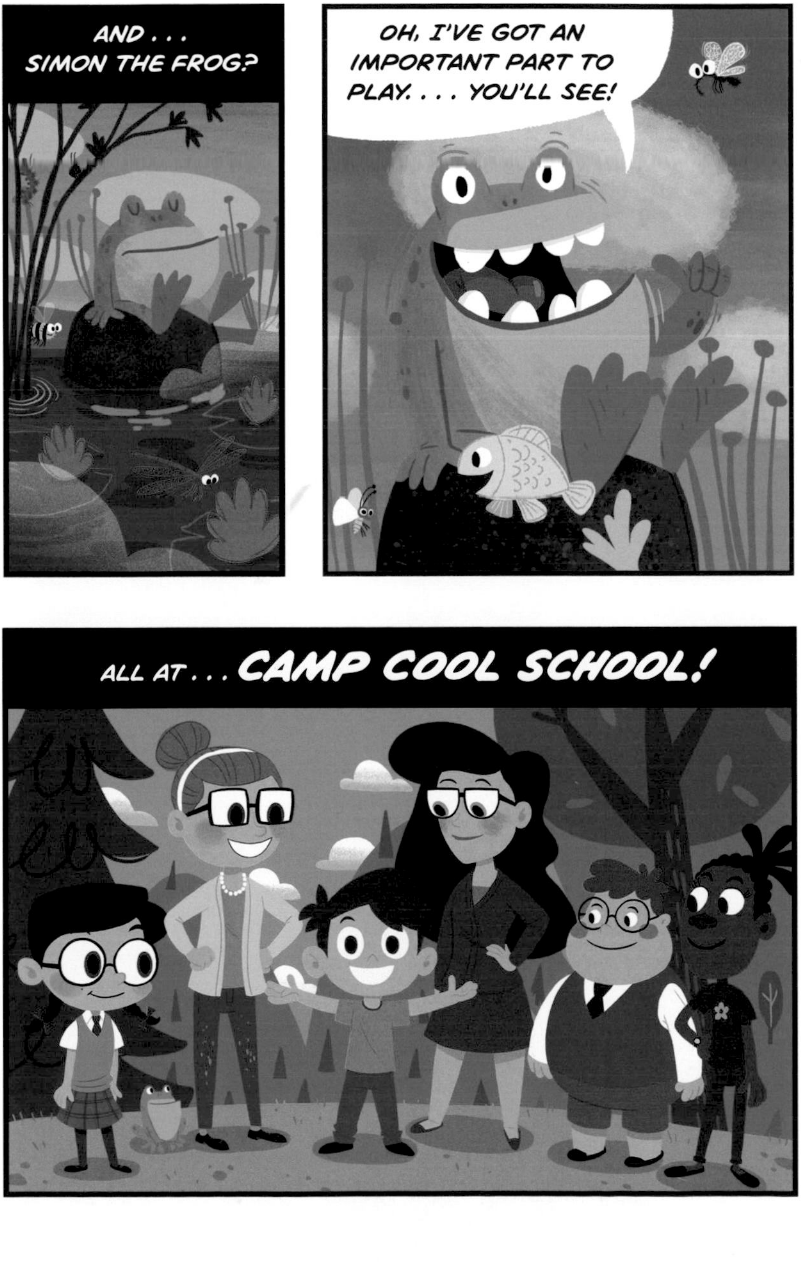
AND . . .
SIMON THE FROG?
OH, I'VE GOT AN IMPORTANT PART TO PLAY. . . . YOU'LL SEE!
ALL AT . . . CAMP COOL SCHOOL!

Drew was superexcited. On the last day of Camp Cool School, all the campers wore blue. They were ready for . . .

the COLOR WAR!

A color war was when one team wore one color (like blue) and competed against a team of rival campers from across the lake that wore a different color (like red). There were lots of contests, and whichever team had the most points at the end of the day won the color war.

Dressed in blue, the Camp Cool School team members met on the morning of the color war. Drew used his Pen Ultimate, which magically brought everything he drew to life, to dress himself in his blue superhero costume.

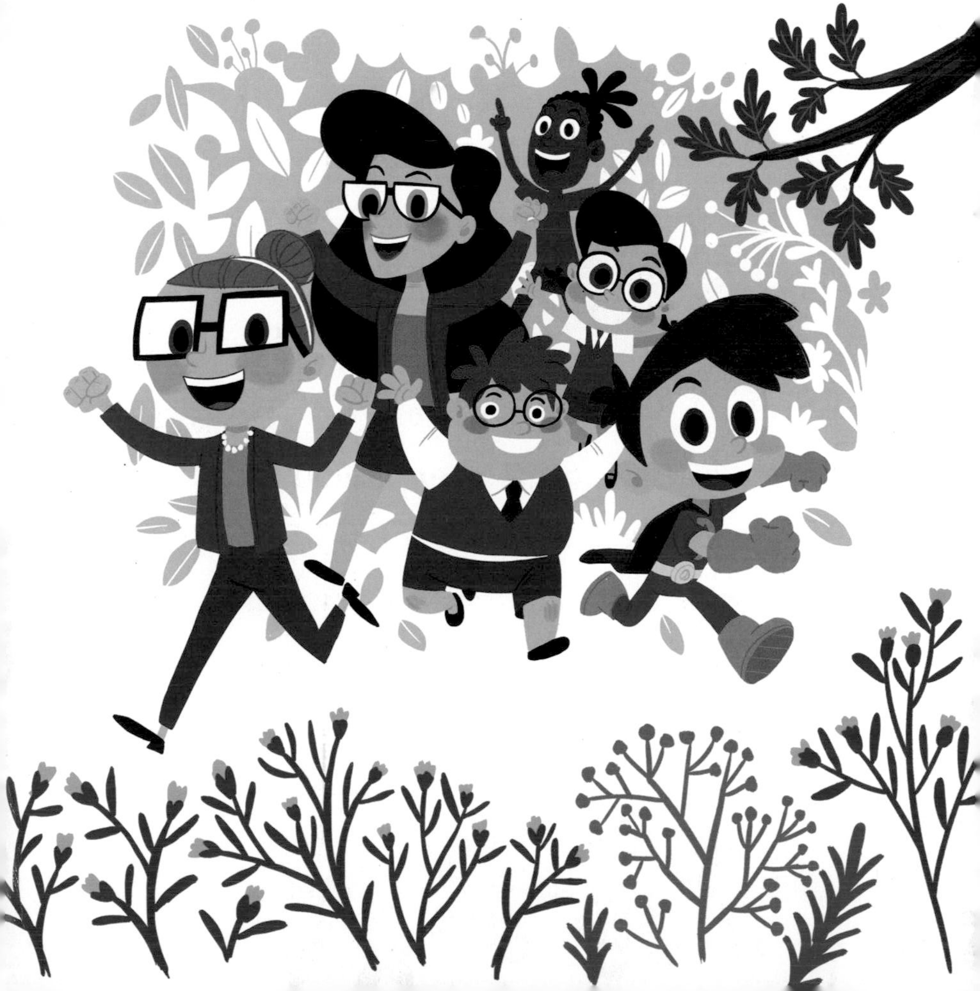

"Okay, Team Blue!" Drew said. "We've never met these campers, so we don't know how big they are."

"Or how crafty," added Crafty Carol.

"Or how smart," Nikki chimed in.

 But Drew wasn't worried about the other team. Not one bit. "I KNOW we can win," he said confidently. "Team Red's got nothing on us!"

Everybody cheered.

"Wait," Nikki said, looking around. "Where IS Team Red?"

"Here we are," said a familiar raspy voice. "Ready to play?"